SON OF
PETE FLUDE

I dashed headlong into the road, not mindful of the danger, and flagged down the first car that I saw. Luckily it was only going slowly. The driver, a man, leaned across the front seat and said through the open window, "What's wrong, sonny?"

I don't know what I replied but it was probably garbled. Something about being chased, kidnapped, drugged. "Okay," he said. "Get in the back."

I almost fell into the back of the car. It seemed like luxury. Soon I'd be home. But the relief didn't last long. Instead of screeching away from the place to the nearest hospital or police station, the driver spun the wheel and the car lurched on to the track up to the junkyard. "Where are you going?" I shrieked. He didn't answer. I yanked desperately on the handle but could not open the door. "Don't bother," the man said. "Child-proof locks."

Point

SON OF PETE FLUDE

Malcolm Rose

◼SCHOLASTIC

Scholastic Children's Books,
Scholastic Publications Ltd,
7–9 Pratt Street, London NW1 0AE, UK

Scholastic Inc.,
555 Broadway, New York, NY 10012-3999, USA

Scholastic Canada Ltd,
123 Newkirk Road, Richmond Hill,
Ontario, Canada L4C 3G5

Ashton Scholastic Pty Ltd,
P O Box 579, Gosford, New South Wales,
Australia

Ashton Scholastic Ltd,
Private Bag 92801, Penrose, Auckland,
New Zealand

First published in 1991 by Andre Deutsch Limited

This edition by Scholastic Publications Ltd, 1994

Copyright © Malcolm Rose, 1994

ISBN 0 590 55721 1

Typeset by TW Typesetting, Midsomer Norton, Avon
Printed by Cox & Wyman Ltd, Reading

10 9 8 7 6 5 4 3 2

Acknowledgements

With thanks to the music publishers and musicians listed below for permission to quote excerpts of their copyright lyrics, and particular thanks to those musicians who allowed their lyrics to masquerade in these pages as the work of Pete Flude. I would like to acknowledge the patient assistance of the Music Publishers' Association, and the inspiration of The Chills, James, Nick Cave and The Bad Seeds, The Waterboys, The Cure, and Kitchens of Distinction.

Sources of Copyright Lyrics Quoted by Permission

pp. 68 and 79 *The Best Years of Our Lives* by Steve Harley and Cockney Rebel.

Written by Steve Harley. Published by Trigram/Rak Publishing Ltd, 1975.

p. 181 *Plain Sailing* by Tracey Thorn.
Written by Tracey Thorn. Published by Complete Music Ltd, 1982.

p. 187 *River of Money* by The Go-Betweens.
Written by Robert Forster and Grant McLennan. Published by Complete Music Ltd, 1984.

pp. 65, 98, 101 and 200 *Frankly Mr Shankly* by The Smiths.
Written by Morrissey/Marr. Published by Morrissey/Marr Songs Ltd, Warner Chappell Music.

Thanks also to the following authors and publishers for permission to include copyright material. Vladimir Nabokov, *Lolita*: Copyright 1971 by Article 3C Trust under the Will of Vladimir Nabokov. All rights reserved. Used by permission of the Estate of Vladimir Nabokov and Weidenfeld & Nicolson Ltd. Albert Camus: *The Outsider* (published abroad as *The Stranger*): Copyright 1942 by Albert Camus, translation by Stuart Gilbert, Copyright 1946 by Hamish Hamilton Ltd, London.

Chapter 1

Good day, sport.

Well, how do you start a novel? Or autobiography. Originally, I started with, "You are about to witness the story of the destruction of a schoolboy and . . ." You know what my tutor, Miss Greene, said? "It's pure sensationalism, Seb. You're not writing for *The News of the World*, you know. You're doing it for yourself. You're the type to want more than cheap thrills, particularly if you're serious about making it into a real novel." So, how should I start it? "It's your story," she said. "You decide. But the beginning of a novel should grab the reader's attention and be unique, original. Maybe see the central character just before a big scene or a situation of conflict. Why not look at a few classics and see how they did it?" One of the startling beginnings that I found in the library was by someone called Camus. It goes, "Mother died today. Or, maybe, yesterday; I can't be sure." Now that's a great goal within seconds of the kickoff. I wish that I'd thought of it. But does it invoke sympathy, like an own goal, or curiosity? At this stage in my story, I'd settle for curiosity. Then there was *Lolita*. I'd heard of this one. "Lolita, light of my life, fire of my loins." Strong stuff for starters, eh? "My sin, my soul. Lo-lee-ta: the tip of the tongue taking a trip of three steps down the palate to tap, at three, on the teeth. Lo. Lee. Ta." But, hell, I can't write that literary stuff. Besides, neither Sebastian nor Lisa trips off the tongue like Lolita.

Any further hints from Miss Greene? "No. Just keep off the destruction bit. No one will deny that you've had it rough – to say the least – without your ramming it down their throats. Understate, Seb, rather than overstate. And another thing," she added. "Don't start with your usual catch-phrase, whatever you do." "How do you mean?" I asked. "You know. Your usual greeting of 'Good day, sport'." "Why can't I put that? It's certainly unique and original." "Well, for one thing, they'll think you're Australian."

So there you are. You now know something about me. I'm either a rebel or a joker. Or both. But I won't say which. You can decide for yourselves as my story progresses. Anyway, a man has to retain his mystery, doesn't he? I should add, though, that I'm as English as they come. And, as you've realized, my name is Seb. Sebastian! Have you ever heard of such a name? There again, what would you expect from a father like mine? I suppose I should be grateful that he wasn't a football fan. He might have given me the names of all eleven first-team Sheffield Wednesday players. I guess, though, that Mum would have stopped him – she was the one with the sense in our crazy family. But enough of them for the moment. They have their proper places in the story – it's as much about them as me really – but not here. Another Miss Greene tip was not to introduce too many characters early on.

So back to me. I guess that you could call me a schoolboy. Seventeen years old, still living in Sheffield. I was fifteen at the beginning of the story (autumn 1985) and in those days I lived in a house – a big one. Detached, with a large garden that led directly into a wood. It's in the wood that I'm really going to start the story. In a moment. There's one important fact about me that overrides all others so I'd better spell it out right from the start, even before we progress to the conflict in the wood. It'll be clear to you if I tell you that my full name is Sebastian Flude. A couple of years ago, the conversation may have gone like this. "An unusual name, Flude," you'd have said. "And doesn't Pete Flude live in Sheffield? You're not . . . are you?" "What?" I would reply, pretending I didn't know what you meant. "Related to Pete Flude?" "No," I'd shake my head. "No real relationship. He's just my father." If you're female, you'd have thought for a bit, then decided on hysterics. "Pete Flude! He's wonderful." Let me assure you, he was as mortal as the rest of us. "Surely he's not old enough to have a teenage son." He was. Easily. It was through the modern miracle of cosmetics that he looked as he did under the camera. The immortal pagan look was painted on. Without make-up, he looked thirty-odd – thirty and quite a lot – married, one kid (yours truly), looked haggard in the morning, got his socks as smelly as the rest of us. I remember some starry-eyed female journalist saying in a rare interview with Mum, "It must be great to be married to Pete." Mum replied, "You don't have to wash his pants and socks."

Don't get me wrong again. (I recall the Australian misconception.) Mum loved him all right. Very much, I reckon. But she had a sense of proportion, even scepticism, when it came to stardom. Not to mention a good line of defence against journalists who pry too much.

Journalists hardly ever got close to Mum, and I never got interviewed at all. Dad protected us from publicity. Or did it not suit Dad's image as an angry young man to be seen to lead a family life with a conventional wife and conventional grown-up son? I might have been asked, "Isn't it great having Pete Flude as your dad?" In those days I'd have replied, "Who?" Then perhaps a jolly little tale to express how good it was to have the front man of Afterglow as a father. It could be any one of a number of examples, most concerning girls. Lisa Woodward, say. In this particular case, the exchange, as I recall, went like this.

"You're Seb Flude?"

"That's right."

"Flude as in Pete Flude?"

"'Fraid so."

Lisa jumped up and down in glee, clasped her hands, virtually dived on me. "Yes, sure I'll come out with you."

She drank, danced, chatted with me all evening. Never left my side. You know why, don't you? But, I lived in hope. This rather gorgeous girl might just be after me myself. It was a big date for me. I was keen on Lisa. Anyway, back to the events of that night. After the gig, off we went, under the railway bridge and past the two druggies sitting underneath it (more of those silly buggers later), to Middle-wood cemetery. It was all dark and there was a full moon. (Must be a mistake here. Cock-up on the memory front, as they say. Perhaps it was fairly dark with a full moon that wasn't so bright.

Anyway, it was your real Mills and Boon romantic setting. Undoubtedly promising.) We tried to suppress giggles at the enamoured grunts and groans going on in another part of the cemetery. Went into a full body clench with Lisa. Kissed her. She seemed to enjoy it at the time. Just when I was beginning to think that it was my night, she disengaged. Damn! "Just a minute," she panted. She shrugged my hands off her shoulders and began to undo her blouse. Perhaps, I thought, it is my night after all. Into the land of the grunters and groaners myself. She undid most of the buttons then smiled at me coyly and turned her back. Like some modern-day female Houdini, she extracted her bra without taking the blouse off. (I'm still trying to figure out this clever manoeuvre. She pulled it out from one of her sleeves – I think that's the key to the trick. Anyway, the bra was extracted – like a rabbit from a hat.) Then ... Horrors. She buttoned up her blouse again before turning round to face me. There was an irresistible, mischievous sparkle in her eye. "Here," she said, handing me her horribly warm bra. "Could you get Pete . . . I mean, your dad, to sign it for me? Both cups, mind."

Now you know what I had to put up with. It wasn't an isolated case, either. I've received pants, plain, white, sexy black (come on, girls; how could he have written on silky jet black ones?), big, little, minute, ones with a naughty slogan across the front. All sorts. Then there was the converse, "Yeah, sure, Seb. I'd love to come out with you tonight. I think I can make it, if . . ." If what? "Well, can you bring me one of his shirts? Or a signed photo?" They asked for anything – grotty old pants, and those sweaty socks again.

Yes, I would have probably enjoyed telling it all to a journalist. *NME*, I should think. They didn't like Afterglow so they'd have printed it. If you asked me the same question now – "What about Pete Flude as a dad?" – you'd get a different response, of course.

But here I am, holding up the real story. Even when I promised to start just before a big scene. So let's get on with the whole painful ordeal – painful for me to recall, I mean. But I think I'm supposed to feel better after I've poured out my soul to these bits of paper. We'll see.

The wood at the back of the house was a bit odd. It was on quite a sharp slope in places and at the bottom of the hill there was the railway. Busy line, Sheffield to Manchester and the London line. The wood ran, long and thin, alongside the railway line. In area, it was quite a large wood, considering it was inside Sheffield city boundaries. (Our whole area was very leafy and "pleasant". You know, middle to upper class pleasant. Reserved for posh people. One of the few areas in Sheffield that always elected a Tory councillor, despite Dad's vote.) Anyway, the wood was entirely unruly – looked as if it had been thrown together in a hurry, or maybe on a Friday afternoon by council workers. All sorts of trees banged up against each other, almost impenetrable in places. Then, towards the bottom, the trees were less dense and separated by hard-packed earth. That's where the rich kids rode up and down the slopes on bikes. There were lots of wood pigeons, owls, magpies and squirrels. By all accounts, there was quite a community of urban foxes too – everyone but me had spotted them. All in all, it was an adventure playground that I always loved.

Being on quite a slope, you couldn't just wander anywhere in the wood. There were three main paths running parallel to the railway. One at the top, one in the middle and . . . you're way ahead of me . . . one beside the railway at the bottom. But coming and going to school I steered clear of these motorways. I had my own byroads that most travellers didn't even know existed. It was on my way home from school on one of these obscure paths that my life began to get complicated. In autumn, the wood looked its best with colours of orange, green and brown. It was just getting dark. (I can't help this horror movie cliché. It *was* getting dark just as the nastiness began. It's not my fault that it's unoriginal. In fact, somewhere an owl was hooting rather early but I'd better not dwell on it or you'll think I'm making it up or simply copying that scene where the unknowing innocent girl makes her way towards Dracula's castle just as darkness is falling.) Back to the serious stuff. I was strolling along, wading through dead leaves, singing Afterglow's latest quietly to myself. I couldn't help liking it – Dad had really pulled his finger out this time.

> *Night has fallen.*
> *Inside*
> *fires are burning*
> *warm and bright.*
> *Secure.*
>
> *God-forsaken.*
> *Outside*
> *wind is sighing*
> *cold and dark.*
> *Street lure.*
>
> *A baby cries.*
> *A child dies.*
> *Journalists moralize*
> *Politicians patronize*
> *And mother*
> *she stares with Cocaine Eyes.*

*   *   *

Then, above the rustling of the leaves, I heard something moving about. I stopped and turned round. There was a squirrel looking at me, almost impishly. It's my path more than yours, he seemed to be saying. I smiled and took a step towards him but he darted off and up the nearest tree. My eyes followed him only until he reached a fork in the tree, about seven feet up. As the squirrel dashed to safety in the heights, I found myself squinting at the nook in the tree where a bit of a paper bag or something was poking out. I'm not the tallest bloke in the world, so I had to stretch on tiptoes to reach it. I just touched the corner of the paper (I could feel that it was indeed paper) when I heard yet another noise behind me. Much louder this time. Someone, or even two people, running towards me. I came down off my toes and turned to see what was going on. I didn't have much time. I certainly saw something long and thickish. A branch, I suppose, just before it crashed down on me. I didn't see the man – or even decide if it was a man, or more than one man. Thinking about it afterwards, I guessed that he, or they, had been going to collect this thing in the tree when he heard me coming, rustling and singing. He must have ducked behind a tree till he saw that I had spotted his treasure. Then he decided to act.

The sceptics amongst you may be reminded of those monkeys that are trained to climb trees and throw down coconuts. You'll be saying, Seb's squirrel shot up the tree, plucked an acorn and hurled it down on the poor weedy fellow. The blow on the head caused him to hallucinate about it afterwards. Besides, no one would admit to being knocked out with an acorn. Either that or Seb's been on one of those substances that Afterglow's drummer got arrested for possessing. I deny both.

I seemed to be out cold for an age but in fact it was only a few minutes. Even so, my head never felt so bad. I thought my skull had broken. When I came to, I was sick all over the place. And, yes, the thing in the tree had gone.

Chapter 2

Well, okay, I admit it. Not the acorn or illicit substance theories, but that it wasn't such a big scene. I promised you a big scene and I gave you a crack on the head. But it was important to me, do you see? A big scene for me because it marked the beginning. In the most striking way possible. But seriously, it was important enough for me to consider writing it in the third person. You know: he did this; he did that; his head was hit as if by a sledge-hammer. I thought that I could distance myself from the event – and all subsequent events – like that. I would have welcomed the detachment. But the story came out cold and false like that. I couldn't regard it as *me* although it was me. I knew then that I'd have to get involved in it all over again. But there are ways of protecting oneself without inflicting the misery on some poor, innocent and purely hypothetical third person.

So there I am, creeping into the house, scuttling through the kitchen, tiptoe in the hall, foot onto the second step of the stairs (the first one creaked) to climb surreptitiously up to my room and safety, when out of the studio strolls Dad. The megastar – never at home when you want him, always on the road or away recording – appears when you least want to be seen by him. "What," he asks articulately, "the bloody hell happened to you?"

It was one of those occasions when "Nothing" just does not suffice as a reply.

"Ah, I was hoping to slip upstairs and clean up before being seen."

"That doesn't tell me what happened – just that you're ashamed of it."

"Or brave, Dad. That's it!" I said. "I saw this toddler step off the pavement in front of a number 26 bus. I – the hero – ran into the road just in time to push him out of the way, and took the full force upon myself."

"I hope he was grateful."

"No. There was a lorry coming the other way."

Actually, my smile was weak and Dad knew it. I must have been in pretty poor shape. I knew that my hand on the banister was trembling and my stomach still felt queasy. Dad came over and took my hand to guide me safely down the stairs. (Yes, he actually touched me. Quite comforting really.) He must have realized that I was light-headed. "Come on," he said. "I'll clean you up." He put his arm round my shoulder, led me back into the kitchen and sat me down on a chair. He was rummaging in my hair as if looking for fleas. I couldn't feel his fingers at all. Either he used a very light touch or the top of my head was numb.

"Water and Dettol needed. It's a bit mucky on top. And quite a gash."

"Have you seen the size of a number 26?"

Dad was dabbing at my mucky bloody head – and he really did do it delicately, obviously he missed his profession because he was never that deft with six guitar strings – when Mum emerged from the lounge. "Pete?" she called. Then she saw us, nit-picking in the kitchen. "What's going on?" she asked, half surprised, half panic-stricken.

"Now," Dad whispered in my ear, "here's Mum. The truth will out."

He was right. I couldn't joke my way round Mum and I couldn't prolong her agony. Well, worry at least. So I told them all. It didn't take long; there wasn't much to tell. But during the telling Mum cast several probing, anxious glances (maybe even frowns) at Dad. At the time, I interpreted her expressions purely as motherly concern. When I eventually escaped Dad's clutches, the rest of the evening was rather frosty. And after I retired to recover in my room, I could hear muffled, heated exchanges downstairs. Odd, but not odd enough to arouse my suspicions. Or perhaps the blow on the head had stunned for a while my imagination and inquisitiveness. It had certainly made me soft – I'd enjoyed the rare event of being pampered by Dad.

Whilst I'm thinking of the bedroom scene (don't get hopeful – it's not that sort of bedroom scene), let me mention my hi-fi equipment. It was stacked in my room and I was the envy of the whole school. Now, I love music but I also had this problem – called Pete Flude. He bought the system for me. I should think we're talking in the realm of 0.1% of the proceeds of the last single. Presumably he was trying to foster an interest in rock music, like a carpenter buying his son a saw. Anyway, back to my problem. I would bring home a record or tape and get one of two reactions. "Oh, you'll like that. Bill's all right. Knows what he's doing in this game." It was almost an order to like it. The other reaction was, "My God, not that! Masters of the one-fingered keyboard solo. Not an ounce of brain between them. Hyped trash." An order not to like something. For a while I tried to like the trash and hate what he told me was good but it didn't work out. You can't dictate your taste either way.

On the night of the blow, I put on a favourite tape. It helped me forget that there was something going on down below between Mum and Dad. I listened to the cassette and looked out of the window. At the time I didn't realize that something might be going on outside as well. I saw it but didn't recognize it as anything but ordinary. I wonder now about lots of other happenings too, of course. How many apparent trivialities had a significance that I failed to recognize?

Well, there I was in my room, gingerly feeling my sore head and admiring my favourite tree. Actually, I should note that my bedroom was at the front of the house so the window overlooked the road. I've already said that we lived in a leafy district. Our road was lined with trees too. Some twenty-five metres to the right of the end of our drive was a wonderful lime tree. There was nothing special about the tree itself, especially in daylight, but there was a yellow streetlight immediately behind it. The lamppost was hidden from my view but the glow from this invisible source illuminated my tree. At that time of year it was at its best because the yellow glow penetrated the thin dying leaves and gave them a new luminescent life. (There, Miss Greene, I'll make a novelist yet.) The shimmering leaves always reminded me of a mass of Chinese lanterns, decorating the night air. It's sad that I'll never see that effect again. Anyway, a man strolled up the road, stopped under my lime tree and took out a cigarette. Another man, walking in the opposite direction, also stopped. This second chap took something out of his pocket – a box of matches – and, all the time chatting to the man with the cigarette, lit it for him using cupped hands. Another Chinese lantern, this one lighting up the smoker's face as he dipped towards the flame. He inhaled deeply then let a long stream of smoke flow from his lips. He nodded to the man with the matches, presumably signifying his thanks, and then continued to wander up the road towards our house.

At that point, a huge grey moth thudded against my window, determined to batter itself silly. I confess that I can't stand moths – those dull, dusty, stupid ones that can't tell the difference between a light bulb and the moon. I was certainly not going to let it sleep through the winter in my bedroom, so I quickly drew the curtains. Besides, I didn't want the man outside to notice me spying on him.

The whole episode was innocent enough, I think you'll agree, but now I can see all sorts of implications. How blind and innocent I was then. Perhaps not unlike the virgin headed unknowingly towards Dracula's castle after all.

In the morning my lumpy scabby head felt more than nine hours older, but no wiser. And the bad news for Mum was that it had leaked a bit into the pillow. Some biological action was called for. Downstairs, the living room smelled of stale cigarettes. Very odd. (Mum and Dad didn't smoke, you see. At least not tobacco. They weren't averse to smoking a certain something but the smell wasn't right for that.) Over breakfast, I asked, "Who called last night?"

"How do you mean?" Dad replied guardedly.

"Cigarette fumes in the lounge."

"All right, Sherlock. Andy dropped by, that's all."

I felt as if the tables were being turned on me. I had joked my way past Dad's autopsy last night, now he was doing it to me. Mum's quiet acceptance of his comment was just too quiet. Her frown told me that she did not approve of Dad's dodging the issue but was not prepared to overrule him and spill the beans. It was a tense breakfast, only the crunching of Branflakes and Alpen broke the icy silence.

Reading back over these last few paragraphs, I think that I might have introduced another couple of misconceptions. Mum and Dad weren't fanatic pot-smoking silent types. Let me explain. M & D were teenagers in the sixties, so what can you expect? We were your actual liberated household. Very fond of pot plants, if you know what I mean. Occasionally they did partake of the dubious pleasures of pot. It helped them relax, they said. And they were quite happy to talk about it. "Pot" wasn't a four-letter word, if you see what I mean, in our house. Neither was sex, glue, heroin, pornography and the rest of it. They were open to discussion on anything. Such openness seems to take away the attractions of such things, or most of the attractions, if I'm anything to go by. At school, the offspring of the local accountants and executives were all rebelling against their parents who wouldn't let a single word in my list pass their lips, at least not for discussion with what they hoped would be life's future stockbrokers, etc. Hence their kids got attracted through curiosity to all things considered as naughty. Ripe for the fads and the pushers. Several were getting stuck into the glue craze, and smoking this and that. There were even two lads (the couple sitting under the bridge, if you remember) on heroin. In contrast, I was a dead loss at the vices, even though I was expected to be an expert because of my liberated family. Let me illustrate my innocence. The following once happened in a small stationery shop. "I can't see your Tippex. Have you got any?" I asked.

"Yes, keep it behind the counter. What do you want it for, sonny?"

Don't you just hate people who call kids "sonny" – and ask ludicrous questions? "Er, paint my bedroom ceiling with it."

"Sonny. . . !" he said, in a sort of school teacher's warning tone.

"OK. I give in. I'll tell the truth. I had this crazy notion that I could use it to erase mistakes in my homework and write something else over them."

"You weren't intending to do anything silly with it just because there's solvent in it, were you?"

"Oh, I see." I really hadn't twigged till then. "You think I'm a secret Tippex sniffer." So you see, I really was innocent. Despite all that's happened since, I think I still am. Glue gives me a headache just when I stick things together so that never tempted me, smoking churned my stomach and pot simply made me feel unpleasantly drunk. And hard drugs – the less said about them, the better. I know what they can do. I must say that I like the odd illegal drink or two but really I get so bloated after a couple of pints that I'd rather drink fruit juice. But I'm entirely off the point. It was supposed to be a section on M & D and it turned out to be about me again. I guess I'm just trying to make the point that I was regarded as something of a loner, an outsider amongst my mates at school. Anyway, I was allowed to be a little eccentric – it was expected of me, being the son of Pete Flude. In fact, it seemed to be the feeling at school that anyone related to the said megastar couldn't be an ordinary human at all. But the second point of this paragraph is that the Flude household wasn't a den of iniquity, full of unbalanced, demented characters – that was just Dad's stage act. Mr and Mrs Flude were simply honest and open about things, that's all.

"Get on with the story!" I hear you cry. That's a metaphorical cry, of course. I still do hear noises though, even voices sometimes, in my ears – after all this time – but nothing so coherent as a complete sentence. Now, the story.

Not long after the happenings that I've described, a momentous event prevented further discoveries in the wood on my way home from school: the clocks were put back one hour. (I really don't approve of government interference with time. No good will come of it.) Bonfire night died a death in rainstorms but, judging by the characteristic smell that lingered the next morning, some ardent arsonists managed to dodge the showers and light up their dreary evening. Anyway, having fixed my story in time without listing a lot of boring dates (as Miss Greene suggested), it will be obvious that it was too dark to spot anything in the wood any more. But in the streets it wasn't too dark for ominous discoveries. There wasn't a specific moment at which I became aware that I was being followed home; it was a slow realization. The first man that I spotted wasn't your B-movie actor type in long raincoat and silly hat. He was a fairly young chap in rather worn denims. For a potential child-molester, though, he had quite a friendly face. I couldn't imagine that such a face had unfriendly intentions. (Mind you, if all molesters looked like molesters, I guess they'd all soon get caught.) At first I didn't tell Mum about it – Dad was away at the time, more gigs in the States – because she would only have worried. It wasn't always the same man. And sometimes I didn't see anyone following me at all. Maybe I'm not a good enough spy, or maybe there really wasn't anyone on some days. I don't know. I became convinced that I was being followed *to* school, as well. The faces that I spotted remained friendly and I remained un-molested but as it went on I got more and more paranoid about it. I cracked after one week. I might have been accused of having an overactive imagination, I might have panicked Mum, but I had to talk about it.

Chapter 3

I expected Mum's face to turn as white as a sheet but, no, it went as red as a beetroot. She seemed embarrassed and angry more than surprised. Uncannily casual, she was. "Mrs Flude, your son's being followed around by perverts all the time." She shrugs, "Oh, really. Sign of the times, I guess." Well, okay, she wasn't *that* casual but she sure wasn't rushing to phone the police. In fact, she was quite silent for a while, staring at the floor rather than at me. Eventually she did look at me and said, "I wish your dad was here. He's the one to explain this situation."

Mum was never normally reticent. Dad's frequent absences had taught her to cope with any situation, be it a blown fuse, a burst tyre, a dripping tap or an unruly son. She was not reliant upon Dad. So why now? "You mean that Dad knows what's going on?"

"Yes. Me too, but I can't really go into it without him."

"I see," I lied.

"I'm sorry," she said. "But it's okay. You're not in any danger. In fact, you're well protected."

Protected? Not in danger? Do I need protecting? And is there someone else who *is* in danger?

That night, I'd only been in bed a few minutes when Mum crept in. "Seb," she whispered.

"Yes, I'm awake. Have you come to tuck me in?"

She ignored the joke and sat on the bed. "Your dad and I don't quite see eye to eye about keeping you in the dark." She sighed, probably at her own clumsy expression. "But now you must be told what's going on. I'll get him to speak to you as soon as he returns, okay?"

"Okay, Mum."

Version 1: The ideal ending. Soon after, Dad came home, explained everything, put me out of my misery. Everything was hunky-dory again. End of story. End of novel. That's how I wish I could end the story. But it was nothing like that at all.

Version 2: The truth of the matter. Of course, I knew that events would turn out to be far more complex than version 1. At the time, I even *hoped* for something more intriguing than version 1 – that simple ending would have been an anticlimax. But intrigue has a habit of getting out of hand. So now version 1 does seem ideal. I knew that it wouldn't be that easy because M & D had never kept me in the dark before (remember that the Flude family was open and liberal); it had to be serious. The overheard telephone conversation confirmed it.

But again I run ahead of myself. First came the scrap outside school. Richard (aptly called Dick, being the school's self-styled sex expert – you name it, he'd done it) caught me after school, saying "What's your dad up to, then, eh?"

"How do you mean?"

He waved a copy of *NME* at me. "Arrived late at one of his gigs and forgot his words at another. America is not impressed."

"Oh, *NME* will print anything."

Dick giggled unsavourily. "Bet he was engaging the local beauties at the time."

I must explain that "engaging" was the school's short-hand for enamoured grunting and groaning (get it?). I think it was Dick who first dreamed up this new meaning to the word "engage". Anyway, you can imagine the titters in English Literature when the teacher came up with lines like "Sarah was engaged three times before she finally married" or "The orders are, engage at once." Dick himself had even got to the point of being blasé about engaging – or he pretended to be. The impression that he tried to portray was of someone so experienced that sex was now boring, beneath his dignity. Put all us virgins to shame. As far as my story is concerned, all I'm trying to establish is that Dick was an obnoxious boy.

Your average boy of fifteen would have welcomed the opportunity to show that his dad was a bit of a lad in the sex stakes. But the puritan in me came out again. "Dad isn't like that," I said grumpily.

"Come on!" Dick scoffed. "He's a rock star. All the groupies he wants are there for the asking. He's no saint."

It wasn't so much a real scrap as a lot of posturing, threatening and pushing. (The Fludes were also pacifists.) When things really seemed to be getting out of hand, who should intervene to stop blood being spilled? Not any old passerby, but one of the friendly child-molesters. I recognized the face immediately, but never close up before. Once he'd come between me and Dick, he seemed embarrassed to find himself so close to me. When everyone had calmed down, he backed away rather awkwardly and disappeared into the main street. I never saw that particular face again.

And so to the telephone conversation. It was about three weeks after my chat with Mum. I gathered that Dad was phoning her from Heathrow to announce his return from the States. Mum thought that I was working in my bedroom but in fact I was on the landing, on my way to the loo. I guess that I should not have eavesdropped but I could not help myself, especially when I heard my name mentioned.

"Hi, Pete. You okay? Good tour?"

"Well," she replied to his unheard answer. "You can't win them all. Twelve triumphs out of fourteen is not bad going."

"Well, I can understand that. So you'll sleep it off in London and come back tomorrow?"

"Oh." Mum's disappointment was clear in her tone.

"What does 'Just a few days' mean?"

"So you should be back on Saturday?"

"Okay. Take care, Pete. I just wish you hadn't got into this."

"When you do come back, I've a duty for you to perform. Regarding Seb."

"Seb and . . . the business that's keeping you away for the next few days."

"Look, we must tell him. He knows that he's being watched. These cops aren't as discreet as they said they'd be. He's seen them following him. God knows what he thinks is going on."

"I don't know. What would you conclude if you discovered you were being followed? You'd think you were in danger of some sort, not that you were being protected so, no, I doubt if he knows it's the police. I just told him that he was safe, that's all. It's very difficult, Pete, without giving him the full facts."

"I know your motives, love. You didn't want to drag him into it. But he's been dragged in anyway now, so there's no point keeping quiet any longer."

"A little knowledge is a dangerous thing. We've got to come clean."

"Yes. The whole thing."

"Okay. As soon as you get back. Thanks."

"Love you, too. Bye."

You know, one of the most difficult things about writing this novel is remembering what conclusions I drew from these snippets of information. It's all so clear to me now but it wasn't at the time. Rather than risk giving the game away at this point, I leave you to interpret the one-sided telephone conversation – and all the other events – yourselves. If you understand it all right now, you're more astute than I was at the time. I was downright confused, bewildered even. I suffered then in a more subtle way than the physical suffering that came later. My marks for school-work began to slide, my temper flared the sooner (I refer to the big Dick scrap, for instance – and that was even before the telephone call.) Sometimes I was simply miserable. And Dad's revelations, when they came, did not help a great deal either.

Chapter 4

The few days before Saturday were overcast –
like the proverbial calm before the storm. And
I'm not talking about the weather. But the calmness was only on the surface. Mum was extremely
tense. Clearly, the business that was keeping Dad
from our door was no joke. The façade of normality was continued for a while on Dad's return,
because there was a tradition to maintain. The
glorious home-coming from a tour was always
celebrated by a party at our place. Members of
Afterglow (the ones that weren't sleeping it off,
that is) and various hangers-on would arrive for a
coming-back-down-to-earth party, rather than the
rave up that preceded a tour. The atmosphere was
always relaxed. Andy was exceedingly relaxed (i.e.

smashed) even as he arrived, never mind during the party. Much to Mum's annoyance, quite a few of the bandwagon turned up before Dad.

Dad did arrive eventually, looking a little harassed and full of apologies. Mum and I queued for our hurried greeting before the party consumed him. And what did Mum say? Has it gone well? How are you feeling? Good to have you back, love. No. She said, "Is it over?"

Is it over? What sort of a greeting was that? It carried the sort of cryptic sentiment that I was having to get used to.

Dad nodded and kissed her. I watched and read something else in his face. The reply that I read came with a rider, "For the moment, anyway." I also watched M & D during the party (till I went to bed). Strangely, neither of them joined in the type of relaxation that they'd always enjoyed on these occasions. It was as if they'd lost their appetite for it.

I was the first to surface in the morning. I cleared enough of the previous night's debris for the three of us to have breakfast in comfort, but I correctly suspected that I was in for a far from comfortable breakfast. "Well," Dad said after we'd finished eating and were drinking coffee, "there's no time like the present. I believe I owe you an explanation. And an apology."

I nodded. "So it seems."

"I've . . . er . . ." He peered into his coffee. "It ain't easy, all this verbalization." He was just delaying, of course. Expressive in song, emotions revealed to all – Dad was not one of those men who found it hard to divulge his feelings. He looked up resolutely. "I've been naive, Seb. And evasive." Mum gave a sad smile, but a smile nonetheless. She was pleased that the air was to be cleared. For the first time in ages, her face did not look strained. "On the last tour of the States – not this one, the one before – I was approached by a couple of . . . er . . . dealers. You know what I mean." He paused. "Anyway, we've never hidden it from you that we take pot now and again. We don't regard it as any more dangerous than alcohol, and probably less so. But these dealers . . . reminded me that even smoking pot is frowned upon these days. It turns me, as an influencer of youth, into a corrupter of youth. Or so it's said. And pot today implies cocaine and heroin tomorrow." Dad gulped some more coffee. "To cut a long story short, they said they'd make my activities very public unless I . . . cooperated. Cooperation consisted of bringing back to England a bag of something. Just a kilo or so."

At this point I sighed. It was as if I was the parent listening to the confession of my naughty young child. My mind was racing, making connections. Things were falling into place, all of a sudden. Dad had been recruited by coercion into smuggling, and placed a bag of the stuff in the fork of a tree in the wood, no doubt for the local couriers to collect. But I intercepted the package before they got to it. So, I thought, my head was crunched for the sake of a bit of boring old cannabis. If I'd known what it was, I wouldn't have bothered looking at it twice. "What did you say to their . . . proposition?"

"I told them to sod off."

"Oh." I hadn't expected this. I really thought that he'd submitted to the threats. Though, submitting to that sort of threat would have been stupid. Revelations about Dad's use of pot wouldn't have dented his image that much. It would have been mild compared to the Boy George affair and Phil Lynott's death – both stories that were to break in the coming New Year. But, if my theory about the package in the tree was correct, he had got involved somehow. Not through stupidity, apparently. So how? "Did Geoff persuade you?" Geoff was Dad's manager and image-maker, "He Who Must Be Obeyed", as Dad sometimes called him.

"No. Geoff would regard it as bad for my image to be known as a drug user. But not that bad. No, I got dragged into it by someone else altogether. A young chap, almost as scruffy as me. Anyway, he turned out to be a British cop of some sort. He was working with an American colleague who'd infiltrated a drugs ring that's trying to spread its business over here. The same outfit that tried to twist my arm. The message from this undercover man was that they hadn't given up on trying to get me to smuggle it in. You know all the equipment we have, Seb. These peddlers know it too. Amazing what you can hide in amplifiers, drum kits and speakers . . ."

"And you travel a lot between countries. Very handy," I put in.

"Yeah. I was a good candidate for the job. Too good to let go."

"But why did you do it?" I still didn't understand.

Dad sighed. "The charmer from the Drugs Squad persuaded me."

"What?" For a moment, it didn't make sense. But then it clicked. The British connection. The cop was hoping to follow Dad's consignment and pick off those involved in the British end of the business.

"Before I explain, let me tell you what sort of drug we're talking about. I asked this cop what the gang was smuggling. I guessed heroin but 'No,' he said. 'Not even heroin. We're talking crack.'"

"Crack? That's made from cocaine, isn't it?"

Dad nodded. "The latest craze to sweep the States. Incredibly addictive. In its own super league among drugs. He told me the cocaine's grown in Bolivia, processed in Columbia, supplied to the Bahamas and taken into the States via Miami." Dad did his best not to look crestfallen as he explained, but he failed. "The police know all about that end of the business – the American side – but they don't know who's behind the big push for crack here in Britain. On top of that, they'd like to know the whereabouts of a crack factory that's about to come on-line here."

I had been right. "So you agreed to bring in cocaine so the Drugs Squad could follow it to the factory that turns it into crack and lead them to the British dealers?"

"That's about it." Dad looked at his watch. "Preservation of image and career would be the sceptic's notion of why I . . . cooperated. But it wasn't, Seb. I took the risk because crack frightens me. The Drugs Squad wants to stop the rot, or to stop the rot setting in here at all. So do I. I agreed to give in when I was contacted again."

How do you force someone to do what he doesn't want to do? The dealers were right not to try the lure of big money on Dad. He wouldn't be interested. Instead, they'd gone for the threat to his livelihood. But he didn't fall for it. Pressure from the crooks had not worked. Ironically, he'd succumbed to pressure from the authorities instead. Moral pressure. I could understand Dad being a sucker for an argument based on scruples. He was stirred more by his sensitivity to moral outrage than by greed and fame. All the same, he'd got himself into . . . hot water; that's the dignified fluid to be in, up to the eyeballs. Of course, Dad should have resisted all the pressure, whether it came from the goodies or the baddies. I'd long since grown accustomed to the private fallibility of the publicly infallible Pete Flude but this took some beating. First, he'd submitted to a form of blackmail ("Help us or Britain will be overrun with crack, and it'll be your fault"), then he'd brought the stuff too close to his own home. Still, it could have been worse – his motives could have been as wayward as his actions.

"Risk," I continued. "You mean the risk of the dealers finding out that you were working for the police. There was no risk of being caught smuggling because the police would make sure that the stuff got straight through customs."

"Not quite. You see, they're testing airport staff too. Apparently, cargo can disappear from computer records – with the help of bent airport staff," said Dad. "But you're right about working with the cops. It's out of my hands, though. If the police do their job properly, my cooperation with them won't be noticed."

"Like they followed me so carefully, so no one would notice?"

Mum and Dad glanced at each other. I had touched a raw nerve. "They're more careful when dealing with the big fish, Seb. With the professionals."

"Let's hope so."

"Which brings us to the topic of why you're being followed. You've guessed that it's police protection. I'd better tell you why." He looked at his watch again. "I'll make it snappy because I've got a debriefing session soonish. But I'll come to that too before I'm finished." He pushed away his empty coffee mug and sighed again. "The cop warned me that the first package would be a tiddler. Almost inconsequential. It was a test, that's all. I dumped it, as instructed, in the appointed place out the back," he jerked his thumb in the direction of the wood, "in a tree that you know well. But that particular bag didn't go anywhere. The couriers simply reported to their American chums that I'd been as good as my word."

I interrupted again. "I got bashed for next to nothing."

"Sorry, Seb. The police had a man lurking in the undergrowth somewhere but he couldn't break his cover and ruin the whole operation. He did stop, though, and check that you were okay before he followed the couriers. I was told later."

When it came to a choice between me and an international drugs ring, I knew I was small fry.

Even when the police were unlikely to learn much by chasing a couple of inconsequential couriers with an inconsequential package. "Okay. But there's more to come, isn't there?" I said. "This latest tour, you got another batch, I bet."

"Yeah. I was approached before the tour. A *much* bigger consignment to bring back this time. To Birmingham to be precise. That's where I've been for the last couple of days, making the delivery. A hollow speaker cabinet carries a lot of kilos. And at over £50,000 a kilo, it was a hell of a valuable speaker." He shook his head sadly. "I'd been primed for the job by the police. The night after your bump on the head, a couple of officers came to the house. Remember, you noticed the smell of smoke the following morning."

I nodded. So, he'd lied to me about the police visit. The sins of a father! I chalked up another one. "You told me it was Andy."

"Yes. I'm sorry. Really. I was trying to keep you out of this whole thing, Seb, but . . . Anyway, it's too late to regret that now. They . . . er . . . they told me not to agree to take on the job straight away or the dealer would be suspicious at too willing a courier. I was told to refuse at first, to play hard to get – until they threatened me again. The trouble was that they didn't just threaten *me*. There were threats – and not particularly veiled ones – against you, Seb."

Me? I thought. Why me? I'm just a spectator. Innocent of all involvement. But that's why I was chosen, I suppose. Everyone abhors the idea of a young and innocent victim, especially a father. He'd do anything to protect me, they reckoned. I tried to make my voice seem normal. "What sort of threats?"

"Nothing specific. Besides, there's no danger. I agreed to do the job and the police are looking after you anyway."

Did he believe that? Was there really no danger? I wouldn't say that my minders were inept but I did spot them myself when I wasn't supposed to. And what if this dealer found that Dad was double-crossing him? The whole drugs squad plan would backfire on us – Dad or me, I guessed. Or Mum maybe. Was she under threat?

Dad carried on talking coolly and calmly doing his best to reassure me. The trouble was, he wasn't convincing. Often the more composed he appeared, the more nervous he'd be inside. Before a gig he was super-cool and super-calm outwardly; inside, he was a virtual nervous wreck. Quietness at home meant an outpouring of stress on stage. As we talked, he became more and more passive. He was only just coping with this affair. Despite appearances and cool words, he was scared silly. Like me. "The whole business is nearly over, as well. If the police had their eyes and ears open, they'll have got all the evidence they need. I just have to go off to this debriefing session and that's it."

"Debriefing?" I queried.

"Yes, I'm not sure what it'll be exactly. They just want to squeeze every last drop of evidence out of it – and that includes anything I can tell them."

"How?"

"What do you mean?"

"Well," I said, "you don't just walk into Sheffield's cop shop and announce, 'Here I am, ready to put the finger on Mr Big', do you?"

Dad smiled. He was probably imagining that I was taking it all in good spirits, that good humour implied lack of resentment and fear. Mum knew, though. She was still silent, but she knew how I used humour: to cover up.

"No," he answered. "I've got a strict routine to go through. It will ensure that I'm not followed, or even recognized, as I make the rendezvous."

"You're not going to put on a party hat and clown's nose, are you?"

"Not exactly. But it will keep us all safe."

Us all? So Mum is under threat too. It wasn't a simple case of "cooperate or we'll pull your son's fingernails out one by one" but "cooperate if you value your wife's good looks and your son's young innocence."

For the first time, Mum spoke. "Just be careful, Pete. Subterfuge isn't your strong point. You're

If you've decided to stick with my version of the story, you'll be wanting to know what happened next. The answer is, not a lot. At home, we never talked about the crack business. The topic was too painful, too hot to handle. Globally, nights got clearer and colder, icicles appeared in the wood (hanging from the steep banks over a stream), Halley's comet came and went with much hue and cry, Phil Lynott only saw four days of 1986 – he died from a drugs overdose, the space shuttle blew up, there was a long freezing winter, and in a miserable spring America bombed Libya to make the world safe from terrorism, and Russia contaminated the world with fall-out. Great news, eh? Actually, there was some good news in this period. Dad underwent a change in musical direction. Highly acclaimed, it was. Even *NME* was mildly approving. At the time, I was deeply impressed myself but you may note some scepticism in my present words. I now know what precipitated the change and it wasn't the divine inspiration of musical genius as everyone thought. But I'm racing ahead again. For the moment, let's just chronicle things. First, in the New Year, Dad turned moody. This was a good sign. It meant that a new batch of songs was imminent. The fact that he was more moody than normal at the time of conception was taken to mean that it was a more immaculate conception than normal. Then, the mighty Pete Flude went off to steep himself in black African music. He came back to make an album filled with African choruses and chants, even singing a capella sometimes. A number one album for an age, destined for album of the year, a top-ten single, and even a brief number one single. All, I now realize, inspired by the cunning of a jackdaw.

And me at this time? Well, I never noticed being followed. Either the danger was over or my protector was more efficient. Whichever, it was comforting.

Chapter 5

Really, I shouldn't have described changes in Afterglow's musical direction before describing what sort of band my dad fronted in the first place. So here goes.

Afterglow was something of a cult band once – the sort that only gets played by John Peel. In those days life was less cushy and Afterglow had the respect of relatively few but faithful fans (including Peel). But then the band got promoted to the super league, more or less by accident. It's said that the Falklands War saved Thatcher; it did much the same for Afterglow. On the 1982 album, there happened to be a very relevant anti-aggression song. Geoff, quick to spot a pot of gold, got the record company to release the track as a single.

There were some misgivings: the song could come up against the national pride circulating at the time. But among the kids (i.e. the market) Geoff argued that there was no pride in us being able to beat up young inexperienced Argentinians, quite the opposite in fact. Geoff was, as usual, right. The record-buying public lapped it up, especially after the bad publicity generated by the older generation's complaints about its anti-patriotism. And there you have it. The first top ten hit, riding on the back of the Falklands fracas. Success followed success. And we acquired our large house in Sheffield, replete with studio.

You'll perhaps remember Afterglow's appearance at Saint Geldof's LiveAid charity concert, a performance ranked alongside that of U2's. Both were described as "majestic" by much of the press. With hindsight, though, Dad didn't approve of LiveAid. Its motives were fine but, by presenting a caring and friendly image, rock music had been castrated, he declared. In becoming respectable, rock had lost its raucous voice of dissent and its traditional anti-establishment bite. All the same, after the concert, Afterglow's record sales doubled and Dad stopped complaining about the enormity of Sheffield rates.

And so we came to be settled in Sheffield, a city that boasted among its attractions one Lisa Woodward. I've mentioned that she seemed keener on Afterglow's frontman than on me and had once tried to access the former through the latter. Here was my dilemma: I didn't want to be used by her but I was dying to get off with her. In fact, I was getting quite schizophrenic about the situation. Was I being too suspicious about her motives in occasionally seeking me out? Was I doing her an injustice? The incident with the bra in the cemetery was ages ago. Perhaps she'd changed. Perhaps she *did* like me. Girls can go wild over the Bros brats or Tom Cruise, they're just distant idols – it doesn't stop them loving ordinary mortals. My problem was that the ordinary mortal (me) brought the girl so close to her idol. That was surely dangerous. But what right had I to deny Lisa having an idol? None, of course. So should I succumb, relax my previously pessimistic stance? Or was I just getting desperate? Would *I* be using Pete Flude to get the girl? Let's stop contemplating the issues. Let me simply tell you what happened.

It was a Wednesday evening, about eight. I was sitting alone in a city club feeling a right prune. I'd been let down by a friend so I was just finishing off my drink before going home. You know who came in, don't you? Yes. Lisa. She saw me on my own almost as soon as she came through the door. "Hello," she said.

"Good day," I replied happily. In the surprise of the moment, my pleasure at seeing her took precedence over my suspicions.

"You look a right . . . er . . ."

"Yes," I said, "I feel like a right . . . er . . ."

"Waiting for someone?"

"I was. Dave Simmons . . ."

"Ah," she said, sitting down opposite me.

"You know him?"

"Vaguely."

"Well, you'll probably know that you can always rely on him. He'll always let you down."

She smiled. "What were the two of you up to?"

"Oh, we were going to discuss tactics. We were going to go walking in the hills this weekend. Till one of his mates informed me five minutes ago that he's got flu."

"How irresponsible."

"Yeah. I was looking forward to it. It might be more wellie-wearing weather than walking boots, but it's still nice to get out of the carbon monoxide for a bit."

"True," she said. "I like walking too."

It might have been a miserable spring but the Pennines were still appealing. The National Park within spitting distance of our house was another of Sheffield's attractions. Along with the one sitting opposite me. It crossed my mind that I could try to combine the two attractions into one and ask her to be a Dave Simmons substitute for the weekend, but I didn't. I was still worried about being a Pete Flude substitute myself and, let's face it, a little shy.

"Anyway," I said. "If you weren't here talking to me, you might look like a right . . . er . . . yourself."

"Yes," she said, looking around the room. "I'm here to meet some friends. They don't seem to be here yet. We're going ice-skating or bowling, ten-pin type. Don't know which yet. It's to be decided by democratic means tonight." She hesitated then added, "Hey, why don't you come with us?"

"Well . . ." It was my turn to hesitate. What was best – going home or being with Lisa? "Who are the others?"

Lisa shrugged. "Not sure exactly. There should be three or four of them. All female."

"Ah, well . . ." I wasn't really interested in other girls but the banter demanded feigned, yet clearly playful, interest.

"All feminists, I'm afraid. Lesbians to a man."

"To a man, eh?" I grinned. "I like that. And a great incentive for me to join in. But, I can't skate. And I'm afraid I don't fancy it either."

"We all make fools of ourselves, not just you."

"No. It's not that. I don't mind making a fool of myself. Well, not much. I just don't fancy being totally out of control of myself."

"Yes, I know what you mean. Perhaps it'll be bowling. I'll vote for it, if you like."

You know, she really did strike me as nice. I don't want to turn all soppy but her eyes were bright as if she were anticipating a great adventure with me. On top of that she was easily the best looking girl I'd got that close to. And she hadn't mentioned Pete Flude and Afterglow at all. Even so, my reply was guarded. "Tell you what – I'll come if it's bowling. I'll make a fool of myself there as well, but at least it'll be a controlled foolish performance."

You can probably guess what happened shortly after. Lisa's three friends came in. They said, "It's no good having a vote, Lisa, since we're all in favour of the ice. Okay?"

But can you guess Lisa's reply? I didn't see it coming myself and it staggered me at the time. "Well," she said, "I'm not really bothered about skating. Seb and me were thinking about going bowling together if you're set on skating."

The girls mumbled a bit, probably surprised themselves, then said, "Please yourself," and left.

Lisa looked at me and I looked at her but I didn't know what to say.

"All right?" she asked.

"Er . . . Yes. Fine."

For some unaccountable reason, we both burst out laughing. We had another drink then went to get a bus to Firth Park Bowling Club.

I'd only played ten-pin bowling once before. It

looked incredibly easy, proved incredibly difficult and made my right arm feel like an orangutan's. Lisa had played a few times, so she beat me (quite easily) in both the games that we played. We left Firth Park on the number 17 bus because neither of us would have to change buses in town. The 17 went within walking distance of my house and terminated in Totley Brook, near Lisa's place. It was a long journey, though, because the bus stopped for some time in the city centre before beginning its outward journey. So there we were, sitting upstairs on an almost empty bus, waiting, conversation getting a little thin. It was only a matter of time before Pete Flude made his entrance, as you might say. I was wondering how she was going to wriggle out of her pants on the upstairs deck of a well-lit bus, and whether they'd be an appropriate colour and material for Dad to sign, when the dreaded topic arose.

"I . . . er . . ." Lisa began, but not looking at me, "I owe you an apology."

"Oh, yes?" First Dad, now Lisa. What's this one all about? She was certainly serious about it, her face honest-looking.

"Yes. About us and your dad."

"Oh?"

"You remember. A while ago. I . . . er . . . went out with you for the sole purpose of getting your Dad's autograph from you. I feel . . . guilty about it now. Sorry." She looked at me and added, "I didn't want you thinking I was doing the same again."

I smiled reassuringly. "No, I didn't think that."

"Oh, good. I still love Afterglow but I reckon I'm too old for silly autograph-seeking. It was especially embarrassing because I gave you my bra, didn't I? Still, I've outgrown it now."

We looked at each other for a second and I suppose that a grin appeared involuntarily on my lips. It destroyed our serious conversation. "What am I saying?" she cried. "I meant autograph hunting, not . . ." We both bellowed. The elderly couple at the front of the bus looked around disapprovingly and we giggled the longer for it.

The ice was well and truly broken (and we didn't even have to go skating to do it). I guess you'd say that from that moment Lisa became my girlfriend.

"I was thinking about this weekend," I said as the bus moved away from the Rackhams stop. "Would you like to come to Edale instead of Dave? We were going on the train from Dore. The station must be halfway between your place and mine. We could do a bit of the Pennine Way. Do you know it? There's a pub that does a nice bit of lunch if we want it."

"Yes. Sure. I'd love to."

As we approached my stop, I had to ask the inevitable question. "Do you want to drop in at my place? For a coffee, or something?"

"Well . . . I'm not sure."

"You can if you like. I doubt if the great Dad will be there. He's putting the finishing touches to a new album. Sixteen hours a day. I don't see him either at these times. But I could show you the studio and stuff."

She hesitated. "Another time, eh? I'd love to, but I still feel awkward about your dad."

"You mean you're trying to prove to me that you're not trying to get to meet him through me?"

"Something like that. But look," she said before I could reply, "Why don't you come on to my place this time? You can easily get back on a 17, or Mum might give you a lift, if she's not already in bed."

It wasn't that late so I agreed. "Okay, but I wouldn't want to bother your mum – there's plenty of buses yet," I said, looking at my watch.

Lisa shrugged. "Up to you. Let's just hope that GB lets you in the house."

"What?"

"GB. He's our dog. Originally conceived of as a pet for me but, you know what parents are like in these days of rape, pillage and burglary. He's also a guard-dog. I don't think they'd let me have a poodle even if I'd wanted one. It had to be a big dog. We settled on GB – he's a Rottweiler."

"And what's with this 'GB'?"

"Dad liked GB as soon as we saw . . . correction . . . heard him. He's got an incredibly loud and off-putting bark. But because he was to be my pet, I was allowed to name him. Because of his great volume, I called him Ghetto Blaster. Dad, of course, didn't like that so we compromised on GB but Dad actually calls him GBH."

"I'm not so sure I want to come to your place after all!"

"Well, we're past your stop now, so hard luck. GB's all right. You'll see," Lisa said.

"Okay, I lay myself at your mercy. And GB's, I guess. Anyway," I added, "why did you say that your mum could drive me home? Is your dad disqualified or something? Or has he been mutilated by GB?"

Lisa laughed. "No. Nothing like that. And Dad's clean as a whistle. A car's too important in his line. It's just that he's away tonight."

"You know all about my dad's business. What's yours into?"

"Nothing so exotic or exciting. The opposite, in fact. He's into scrap metal, as they say."

"How interesting! Can I have his autograph on these?" I said, reaching for the belt of my trousers.

Lisa slapped me in play. "Stop it!"

All I can say is that there must be a fair bit of money in scrap. Their house was large and really plush. To many it would look like a palace. Lisa's mother seemed pleasant enough. She didn't throw me out of the house, didn't try too hard to be nice to me either. She was simply casual and ordinary. The atmosphere, though, was more formal than the Fludes'. Everything was very neat and clean. No peculiar smelling fag ends, no beer stains on the carpet, no magazines and books scattered over the tables, chairs and floor. More Sibelius than The Smiths. Or maybe a jazz household. Anyway, I bet the Afterglow albums were confined to Lisa's room. I did wonder what her room was like. Was there a full-length technicolour poster of Pete Flude in frozen action over her bed? (And, no, I never did find out, if you're speculating.)

Even GB turned out to be quite docile and friendly – after a few words from Lisa reassuring him of my good character. Clearly, he'd been trained well because he really did seem ferocious until Lisa calmed him down with those few words. And, yes, he did have a bark like a fog horn.

The half-hour or so at Lisa's was very polite and uneventful. However, we did seal our relationship with a kiss – on the doorstep as I was leaving. I enjoyed the contact. I enjoyed holding her. I guess that I found it comforting after all my recent traumas. I think she enjoyed it too. She certainly clung on. Like me, she didn't seem to want to let go. But the last bus does not wait for ever. I had to run for it. After an evening like mine, the run was more exhilarating than tiring.

Now, what are you thinking? Our Seb's indulging himself in a subplot. Nostalgia, even at the age of seventeen, for good times with Lisa. It isn't like that, I assure you. The Lisa affair is not so remote from the main plot that's preoccupied most of my scribblings so far. Personally, I cannot now distinguish the Lisa Woodward subplot from the main theme, so bear with me. It will not be long before I marry the two. I promise.

The day on the moors was magic. It was also rather wet. We walked, got tired, got muddy and in a remote spot got partially engaged, if you know what I mean. (Even if you don't, I'm not explaining further. There's enough laying bare of my private life and soul in these pages without going into that as well. Let's just say that it was a good job that I no longer had minders watching me all the time.) Mostly, we nattered and got wet. Correction, we got drenched. Don't believe all that "rain can be very sensual" stuff. It isn't. It makes your trousers stick to your legs and eventually your shirt to your body. It's clammy and it's horrible. The only way that it could possibly be sexy is if, as a result, you do away with clothes altogether. (Well, I suppose that would be sensual. Unfortunately, I'm only guessing.)

If there's not a great deal of romance then we

might as well concentrate on the chat instead. Somehow the topic got around to money (can't remember how). Lisa asked how Dad coped with having pots of money in real life and yet, in songs and on stage, identified with the unemployed and the working class. I shrugged. "How does he cope with being old and identifying with the young? It's all beyond me. I think you have to be over thirty to ponder these imponderables. He is rich, I suppose, but you wouldn't know it. If you mugged him on the street, your pickings would be meagre. He never has a penny . . ."

"Does your mum consume it all, then?" Lisa interrupted.

"No," I answered. "She's the same. Never has bothered about money and fame."

"Not even one designer outfit for a few hundred quid?"

"No. Oxfam's more like it."

"Oh, if I were her, I'd indulge a little bit. At least one satin number."

I smiled. "They're not like that. And they don't lavish money on my wardrobe, as you can see." I indicated my muddy, scruffy boots and jeans.

"Mm." Lisa laughed. "I've noticed that."

"Now, don't you start on my dress sense."

"What dress sense?"

"In your present state," I rejoined, "I wouldn't start an argument about clothes."

"No, you're right. I interrupted anyway. You were revealing all about your dad's millions."

"Hardly that. But he wouldn't know what he's worth. All his money is managed for him. Sunk into this and that by Geoff, the manager. Dad probably owns Sainsburys or something but he wouldn't know or care. Geoff gives him pocket money, pays his taxes and things, and tells him when and how and whether to buy anything he wants – like a new guitar or a sofa. He's spoonfed like a baby in some ways. Anyway," I said, as we stopped briefly to lean against a large rock and take in the view, "by the look of your house, your dad's not doing so badly either."

"Not in the same league as yours but, yes, he's doing all right, I guess. Embarrassing, isn't it?"

"You mean, when so many have so little?" Lisa nodded. "Yes," I agreed. "It is. But at least Dad does his fair share of charity gigs, despite having worries that they tame rock music. And he encourages new bands by buying them studio time. He doesn't flaunt his wealth, I'm glad to say. He's just ordinary, really. And he *was* poor."

"Oh?"

"I've seen photos of Mum and Dad living in virtual hovels in the sixties. They looked happy enough. All flowing hair, flowers and flares. Mind you, looking down-and-out and living in dilapidated caravans was the thing then, so I'm told. The first couple of houses I lived in looked awful too but I was too young to remember. The only thing I do remember is that all our houses were filled with music."

"That's not entirely surprising," Lisa said. "I've been meaning to ask you if you play anything. You know, following in father's footsteps and all that."

I grinned wryly. "I'm rebelling, like any son worth his salt, against family traditions."

"Come on," she coaxed. "It can't be as simple as that."

"No, you're right. I feel . . . intimidated by it all. I was encouraged all right, from an early age. At junior school I showed promise, I'm told, in music but the active paternal encouragement got too active and I got turned off by it."

"You know," Lisa said, "I think you're very loyal to your dad really. You like knocking him but deep down . . ."

I remember that I stopped and looked at her, wondering what had brought on such a comment. I shrugged. "He's my father."

Lisa looked puzzled then grinned. "What's that supposed to mean?"

"Doesn't everyone just love 'em and hate 'em? Fathers have their good points and their bad. Mine's no different – just more visible."

"His fans would find it difficult to believe that he has bad points."

I smiled. "I see him from a different angle, in a different light."

"Oh?"

I put my arm around her waist and squeezed. "It's no good prompting for more. We've talked about him for long enough. You won't wheedle any more out of me."

"Ah," Lisa replied. "You are loyal, then."

That was about all that was said about Dad. We did talk about his music a bit, but nothing more. I certainly didn't mention the "drugs problem". I guess that I was loyal to the extent that some things *do* remain sacrosanct within the family. That is, until they're spilled out on paper.

My relationship with Lisa was not in the "torrid affair" category (I'm afraid to say). Nor was it the childish "scratch your name on my arm with a fountain pen" type. (Besides, that went out with Aids.) It was somewhere between the two. Lisa seemed just keen rather than crazed with passion, but caring rather than simply cool and clinical. In other words, I hadn't the faintest idea how I stood with her. Was I supposed to adopt the laid-back approach as well, or was I supposed to jump on her at every conceivable opportunity? If she gave any signals or hints as to the expected protocol, they were so subtle that I missed them. As a result, our relationship, dictated by Lisa, was neither platonic nor steamy. We simply enjoyed each other in a semi-casual, semi-serious, semi-sexual way. Oh, well.

Chapter 6

I promised to bring together the two threads of this story fairly soon. Let the process begin! Actually, in bringing a girlfriend home to meet the old folks, it seems to me to tie a different sort of knot as well. The relationship changes subtly. As if it somehow becomes official by acquiring the parental seal of approval. Maybe it even loses a bit of the thrill, made almost mundane through having official approval. Not really mundane, though, in Lisa's case. Nothing about Lisa was mundane.

Anyway, there we were on the appointed evening, approaching the drive to Flude Acres. "Excited?" I asked, squeezing her hand.

She nodded. "Mm."

"You poor innocent young thing," I taunted. "Is this your first time?"

"Seb!" she warned. "Don't. I'm nervous for all sorts of reasons. Rock stars might be two a penny to you, but not to me."

"I just hope that he doesn't disappoint you in the flesh."

"It's not so much that," she said, "but knowing how to take your dad. The boyfriend's dad, or hero – they seem mutually exclusive, somehow."

Yes, I was thinking, that's what I'm scared of too. "Just take a lead from him. He'll adopt the laid-back approach. Anyway," I said as we wandered up the drive, "no more theory. Here's the practice."

There was no problem, of course. In fact, the evening was great. Mum and Dad seemed to take a shine to her straight away, maybe because she succeeded in treating the almighty Pete Flude as an ordinary mortal, convincing them that she wasn't using me to get to him. Time and events have shown it to be true. As I think back, I can definitely say that it *was* me that she was after. She convinced me then, she convinced Mum and Dad, and she convinces me still.

"Hi," Dad said, half-heartedly getting out of his chair, but not showing any sign of doing something silly like shaking her hand. "It's Lisa, isn't it?"

"That's right. Nice to meet you, Mr Flude."

Dad grinned at the rather awkward formality. "Pete will do. And this is Angie."

"Hello," she said to Mum.

"Have a seat," Dad said. "Oh, just shift those. Sorry." As usual a pile of magazines and papers was cluttering the sofa.

Once the formalities were over, the ice broken, and the meal started, the conversation got around to the rock business. Lisa was right to raise the topic – you can't just ignore a thing like that. "I've . . . er . . . always been an Afterglow fan," she said.

Dad laughed. "I always hoped Seb would go out with someone who had never heard of us, but I'm kidding myself really – I'm glad to hear that fans exist. You've stuck with us, even through all the changes? Surely you disliked something."

"No. It just gets better, especially the latest stuff."

"Mm," Dad replied, less than enthusiastically. "It's not as inspired as people are saying. Could do better."

"Sounds great to me." She hesitated, then said, "Well . . ."

"Yes? Go on. Say it. It's 'The Best Years', isn't it?"

Lisa laughed. "No. That's my favourite. I thought 'Falling at the First Hurdle' was a bit . . . duff."

Both Mum and Dad grinned from ear to ear. "That's *our* favourite!"

"One woman's meat . . ." Mum said.

"What about the other albums?" Dad asked. "Anything duff on those?"

"Now you're teasing."

"True," Dad retorted. "And I bet you're covering up the fact that you don't know the others."

"Not true. I bought them all."

"Ah, that's what I like to hear." Dad turned to me and said, "She's okay, this young lady."

"However, if you invite me again," Lisa rejoined, "I'll prepare you a list of all the duff tracks."

"Cancel that statement," Dad cried. "She's a pain in the bum."

I liked the way she handled him. And Dad enjoyed the irreverent humour.

"Anyway," Dad continued, "you'll be pleased with the news that 'The Best Years' will be the next single."

"I thought you didn't like it," Lisa said.

"It's a rare event when I get to choose the singles. Sometimes I learn which track's been released as a single by reading the music press. It's a business decision, you see, not an artistic one." Dad smiled wryly. "Sickening, isn't it? So much for artistic control."

"Yes, that surprises me."

"I should fight against it, of course. The younger, newer bands do. But when you get as big as Afterglow's become . . ." His voice trailed off. "'This position I have, it pays my way. But it corrodes my soul.' I'm too old for this game. I should stand aside and let the youngsters take over."

"And who," Lisa asked, "are these youngsters who can take over from Afterglow?"

"Oh, I don't know. The Cure maybe, or The Smiths. Morrissey seems to know what he's doing."

"No," Lisa said emphatically. "The Smiths are too samey and The Cure know no middle ground. They're either too wacky or too dreary." That wicked twinkle in her eye that always knocked me sideways was turned on Dad as she added, "Perhaps, though, you'd better watch out for James. I like them." Then, getting serious again, she said, "Now it's me that's teasing. I shouldn't. You love the business. It shows. You don't give up what you love."

Dad smiled. "Perhaps. But rock music continually needs new blood and new ideas. That's what it's all about. And Afterglow isn't going to become an institution like The Stones or Bob Dylan."

Dad was, of course, only baiting her. At least, I thought he was. Despite the sudden sullenness in his voice, I doubted that the "drugs problem" had taken such a toll on him that he'd consider throwing in the towel when, as Lisa rightly surmised, he loved the rock business. He always said that a good song was a good song, irrespective of the writer's or performer's age or status. I hope that I didn't misjudge him here too.

Towards the end of the meal, I asked Dad if Lisa

could see the studio. "She'd really like to have a look."

Not everyone was privileged with being allowed a visit. Dad regarded it as a rather private place. But this time he said, "Sure. You can show her, Seb, while we do the hard labour." He indicated the dirty dishes.

"Thanks!"

Truth be told, I guess that Lisa would have liked to have had a guided tour of the knobs, dials, instruments and electronic gear by the man himself. But Dad was probably conscious of stealing my thunder. Another truth to be told was that the studio was a mess. It always was. Yet Lisa was still impressed.

"Look at the tape recorder. It's enormous!"

"Sixteen track. Hardly ever used now. It's all these." I waved a floppy disc at her.

"Doesn't it all shake the house down when he gets going?"

"No. It's all sound-proofed. You could scream your heart out in here and no one would hear a thing," I said, gripping her shoulders menacingly.

"Stop it!"

"Besides," I said, letting her go, "you'd be surprised how quiet he is, cooking up a new tune. He might be loud on stage but in here it's more likely to be a simple acoustic guitar." I pointed to his favourite one. "Want to hear something?" I asked.

"Oh yes!"

I sat down and took one of the guitars.

"I thought you meant a tape," she said.

I smiled in reply. "'The Best Years', wasn't it?" And I gave her a quick acoustic rendition of her favourite track.

I'm lost now for the words to tell you the truth
Please banter with me the banter of youth

If I knew how to say it I'd say it for you
If I knew how to whisper I'd whisper for you
If I knew how to waltz I'd get up and dance for you
If I thought I could run I'd come running to you

I've discovered now how to be fair
And this I could teach you if only I dare

The only conclusion I've reached in my life
Is that if I should die I should die by the knife
Since it's only a matter of courage all right
Die a man or a martyr, the two would be nice, so nice

You'll think it's tragic when that moment first arrives
Ah, but it's magic, it's the best years of our lives.

It hurts me now to write that one – or at least that bit of it. But it seemed a good idea to give it a whirl at the time. Lisa confirmed it. "That was lovely," she said. "I thought you said you were hopeless or something."

"I am," I replied, putting the guitar down. "I can learn songs parrot-fashion but with me there's no *feeling*. That's what Dad can do. Put heart and soul into it. And, of course, dream it up in the first place."

"Yes," Lisa said thoughtfully. Then, changing the subject, she asked, "Ever been on tour with him?"

"No," I said. "School comes first in this household. Besides, it's incredibly hard work on tour – no time for fun."

"I guess not."

"You've probably been to as many of his concerts as I have. But you watch from the audience while I watch from the stage, seeing all the unromantic bustle behind the scenes. Sheer chaos. Anyway," I added, "what do you think of him now, in the flesh? Has the reality spoilt the dream?" Lisa looked round as if wondering if her reply might be overheard. "You're all right. Remember the sound-proofing."

"Well, I hate to disappoint you, I know how much you'd like me to say that he doesn't live up to expectation, but I like him. True, he looks older than I expected but he's nice. Ordinary, like you say, but also not ordinary. I wouldn't mind him as a father."

I grinned sardonically but didn't reply. "Come

on. Let's go and see if we're safe from the ritual of placing the dishes in the dish washer."

Mum and Dad made themselves as scarce as possible for the remainder of the evening, living up to their liberal reputation. After I'd returned from walking Lisa down the road for the last number 17 bus, both Mum and Dad made favourable noises about her. Made it sound as if she'd passed some esoteric test – with flying colours. Actually, it wasn't so esoteric. M & D knew that I had a potential problem with friends. We'd talked about it in the past. But they seemed to believe that Lisa's motives were above-board, that her first allegiance was to me and not to Dad. Anyway, that night I went to bed a happy lad.

The serenity in the Flude household, though, was short-lived.

One memorable evening, I was watching TV with Mum. It wasn't the thriller that was so memorable, but Dad's entrance. I was feeling pleased with myself over some pretty good exam results so, when Dad came home, Mum kept quiet and let me take the limelight. We anticipated Dad's delight with my news but, in the event, exams never got mentioned.

"Good day," I said, when he entered the lounge.

Dad hardly looked at me. He mumbled, "Yeah," slumped into a chair and muttered, "Hell!"

(Actually, it was worse than "hell" but Miss Greene suggested the change for the sake of good taste.)

"What's wrong?" Mum said, pushing herself forward (figuratively) and barging me off centre-stage.

"I have to come clean again."

"What?"

"Let's have a drink. Then a talk."

A talk! The need for "a talk" shattered my comfy world of grade A in English Lit. and Lang., Maths and Art, B's in everything else, near contentment in my relationship with Lisa, and knowing who'd dunnit in the murder/mystery on the box. "A talk" meant Dad's Danger Man role had risen to the surface again. How?

"My trip to Zimbabwe," Dad confessed, "was not all music and pleasure."

You're probably thinking, "What trip to Zimbabwe?" I mentioned it a while back – this was the trip, at the beginning of the year, that inspired the impressive change in Afterglow's musical direction. I remember what I was thinking as Dad started his confession. "Oh, no! Not an African connection. I'm not sure I can take this." I wasn't sure either what Mum was feeling but she went pale as she listened. Devastated, is my guess.

"But it's got nothing to do with us now," she said. "You've done your bit. Let the cops sort it out. That's what they're paid for, isn't it?"

Dad nodded slowly and sadly. "Yeah. True. But they were getting nowhere. The consignment was put to sleep – meaning it went to ground and didn't surface for an age. Apparently it's a ruse to confound the authorities. Clearly it worked. And this Jackdaw character covered his own tracks just as well, I was told. He slipped the police. Then I was contacted again."

"When?" Mum interrupted.

"A while ago."

"You didn't say anything!"

"I knew you'd be . . . disappointed, love. To say the least. But," he said before she cut in again, "I learned my lesson. That's why I'm telling you now. Before it gets out of hand again."

"Just what's happened?"

"They got me to pick up a consignment in Africa and bring it back here."

Everything was suddenly clear. The Jackdaw's mob was responsible for the album of the year! Dad had been told to make an African connection, he'd turned moody over it (remember?), then dreamed up a musical cover for the trip. The drug squad was no doubt in favour because it allowed them to pick up the scent again.

I'll spare you most of the conversation, which confirmed my immediate conclusions, and fast forward a bit.

"Anyway," Dad was saying, "at least they got back on the trail of this Jackdaw."

"But that's not the end of it, is it?" Mum asked with trepidation.

Dad shook his head. "No. I've just been told. They've been following him since the African trip, but . . . er . . . he's the wily type. Always very careful. It seems that, to avoid losing him again, the police got a little too close to him. This was just the other day. He realized that they were on to him, and the whole thing got out of hand. Guns . . ."

"Oh no!"

"One policeman seriously hurt and the Jackdaw shot – dead."

Neither Mum nor Dad said anything, so I broke the silence. "That's not the end either."

"No, Seb."

"No?" Mum queried.

"Presumably, the drug squad's after your services again. To find a fresh lead," I suggested.

Dad shrugged. "I don't know. I've told you all I know. That's the current state of play. But," he added, "you may well be right, Seb. This gang will be in touch. And I doubt if the police will discourage my involvement. I'm their only lead, I think."

"No more," Mum sobbed.

Yet she must have known as well as me and Dad that the ball was not in Dad's court, but was likely to be returned soon. And she also must have known that, having started, Dad had no option but to continue the game. What none of us knew then was that the ball was to be hit back so hard that it ended up in the lap of a spectator.

Things came to a head one night at the end of May. The whole evening was strained. An ominous cloud hung over it, as you might say. Let's see what went wrong.

I was meeting Lisa in town, to go and see a local band at the Leadmill. First, I lingered too long in the wood. The bluebells were at their best, and several times I stopped to admire the near wall-to-wall decor. I also stopped to gaze wistfully at the tree with a fork in it, wishing Dutch elm disease on it (a forlorn hope since it was an oak). Result: I missed the bus. I turned up outside Virgin Records fifteen minutes late. Luckily, Lisa was twenty minutes late. When I saw her, I smiled and said, "Good day, sport."

"I wish," she replied rather grumpily, "you wouldn't say that. It's silly."

Sorry, I'm sure, I thought to myself. I wonder what's got into her tonight.

"And," she carried on, "your flies are undone."

"Oops," I said, turning my back to the crowds and doing what was necessary. "Trust you to notice," I joked.

I should have known not to crack jokes that night. "I think it's more embarrassing than funny," she retorted.

There was no apology or explanation for her late arrival as we set off for the Leadmill.

What came next? Yes, the band was late. "I really don't fancy hanging around here all night," Lisa said, looking at her watch. "They might be rubbish anyway."

"Dad says they're awful, so they're probably okay."

"Your dad's probably got better taste than you have," she said, rather irritably.

"I see," I said, turning away from her.

For the first time that night, she became herself again. She took my arm, saying, "I'm sorry, Seb."

I shrugged. "What's the matter, Lisa? You don't seem . . ."

"Nothing." She looked down at the floor rather than at me as she said it.

I guessed that it was one of those womanly things that us mere males don't query. Forget it, I told myself. Just one lousy night. Not bad out of a few weeks with her.

It was already late when the band took the stage. We weren't going to catch the last bus if we'd stayed for the whole set, and Lisa got more itchy as time went on, so we left before the band really got going.

Lisa only warmed to me at the very last. A bit before my stop, she said, "I'm sorry I've been such a bore, Seb. I . . . I didn't mean to be. Just one of those things. Not feeling myself tonight."

"It's okay," I said. Then, much to my surprise (and to the other passengers', I guess) she kissed me. Rather passionately. But we were interrupted by a terrific bang somewhere behind the bus. It made us both jump. "What was that?" Lisa asked. Looking back, we saw two cars that had crunched at a junction. "Some silly bugger trying to cross the lights on red by the look of it." Another everyday event that didn't strike me as significant in any way. "Hey, I've got to go, or I'll miss my stop." I stood up.

"Yes," she said sadly, as if regretting that we had no time to make up for a rotten evening.

"See you tomorrow?" I asked as I rang the bell.

"Yeah. I'll get over it by then."

"Okay. I'll call."

Was that the end of the run of bad luck for one night? I'm afraid not. The next thing of note was being kidnapped.

Chapter 7

It was Miss Greene's idea to leave the last chapter at that point. "The reader will be thinking, Kidnapped? Surely not! Really? By whom? Why? How? You see, Seb, no reader could possibly put the book down at that point. Too eager to find out what happens next." Maybe. Maybe you out there are past caring, looking smug because you did put the book down. Well, if you are looking smug, I'm not bothered. You see, I'm not writing this for you. So there! Anyway, I'm going to keep you in suspense yet a while about the kidnap. We'll get to that painful episode soon enough without rushing into it like an SAS raid.

The kidnap ordeal started a minute after getting off the bus and continued through June and July.

But, to satisfy Miss Greene's desire to have all the action put in the context of world events, you'd have been sweltering in a hot June, cheered by Saint Bob Geldof being knighted, bored by Navratilova winning Wimbledon yet again, and dismayed by Sarah Ferguson putting back the cause of feminism by vowing to obey her husband, the once randy Andy, and declaring that a woman should have a trim waist and a fair "up-top" (clearly, she wasn't referring to brains). I only heard of these things later. At the time, I didn't know where I was and half the time I didn't know what I was doing.

Well, I've put it off as long as I can. Let's get on with it.

It was a dark night. I was walking up Abbey Lane towards the house when a car drew up. The window was wound down. "Excuse me," a male voice said from inside the car. I stopped and turned towards him. "Do you know where Hayes Lane is?"

I said, "Er . . ." and didn't get much further. For the second time in one story, I got clobbered over the head. This time, from behind.

Thinking about it afterwards, it wasn't the most sophisticated of kidnaps. Not how it's done in films these days. It should have been the packet of Polos pushed discreetly into my back and the whispered, "Get into the car quietly. No fuss." The principle, I suppose, is that it would have been less suspicious than bundling a limp form into the back of the car. If I was making up all this, I would have portrayed it differently and given it greater subtlety and finesse. But I can only report what happened. It was quite late so there was no one around to witness my limp form being bundled, I guess. And being unconscious, I was less likely to indulge in heroics or cause problems. Anyway, their strategy was effective and the outcome was my abduction. Pure and simple. The grievous bodily harm was merely secondary.

Now, don't go accusing me of using inappropriate humour at this point. You don't know how it feels. It feels painful. Not just physically, but emotionally hurtful. It's an undignified intrusion that makes you feel sullied. I don't presume to know how a rape victim must feel, but I think that I now have an inkling. Outraged, numbed and unnerved, all at the same time. It ain't nice. And because it ain't nice, I have to look back and smile or I'd look back and cry, go mad or something. As I said, I'm writing this for me – to get it out of my system. I need the humour even if you don't.

I've been laughing myself, is that so hard to see?
Do I have to spell each letter out, honestly!
If there's no room for laughter there's no room for me

You'll think it's tragic when that moment first arrives
Ah, but it's magic, it's the best years of our lives.

Now, where was I? Ah, yes. The second crack on the head. At the time, of course, I had no idea where I was when I woke (or came to). You know that feeling when you wake in a strange place and for a few seconds, or minutes at most, you don't know where you are. Well, it was like that. I felt disorientated and panic-stricken. I told myself that it would pass in a few seconds or minutes at most, that a familiar pair of curtains or a wall would come into focus, and that I could be myself in familiar territory again. But I waited a good ten minutes and the feeling of insecurity was still with me. It scared the (how shall I put it politely?) stuffing out of me.

It was dark, very dark, but I didn't know the time. My watch was no longer on my wrist. I guessed that I had lost it in the scuffle. I hoped that it was lying on Abbey Lane pavement as a clue for someone to find. Anyway, my biological clock told me that it was early morning but there was no hint of dawn in the darkened room. No hints reached my ears either. No cars revving up, no birds singing. Nothing. I was lying on a mattress, close to the ground. I realized that it wasn't a bed at all, just a mattress on the floor. I put out a hand and felt a wooden floor – bare floorboards with, it felt, quite a bit of dirt. I wiped the grittiness off my hand on the edge of the mattress and levered myself into a sitting position, my head and back resting against a wooden wall. Hell, I thought, I've woken up in someone's garden shed. But that could not be. Not unless it was still the dead of night. Garden sheds have windows and chinks between the slats, so where were the shafts of sunlight? Besides, I had the impression that it was a larger room than your normal garden shed. There was also a strange smell. An antiseptic type of smell.

I swallowed, then called out tentatively, "Hello?" It came out as a virtual whisper but, in the silence, sounded like a shout. The room gobbled up the sound and silence returned. I cleared my throat and tried again. "Is anyone there?"

The room's silence and anonymity intimidated me. I felt guilty for the disturbance I was causing. (Like the rape victim who, I hear, can begin to feel guilty just for being there, for making herself/himself available for the crime, as it were.)

I decided to undertake another intrusion on the room. I got to my feet, at first rather unsteadily on the mattress itself. Stepping off it was like leaving firm ground to tread on thin ice or leaving the safety of the beach to paddle in shark-infested waters. I guess that I should have felt my way around the walls first – to define the edges of the puzzle as in a jigsaw – but I took off for what I guessed would be the centre of the room. I really don't know how the blind ever get used to the blackness and absolute uncertainty of their world. Each step was taken tentatively and I waved my arms around like a demented singer of a Gothic rock band. My first encounter was with a chair – a dining room type of chair. My introduction to the chair took the form of a painful rap across the knuckles on one of my sweeping arm gestures. I grabbed the back of it with both hands. It felt solid, ordinary and reassuring so I held on to it while I recovered from the shock of finding it.

The logical thing to expect with such a chair is a dining room table. Indeed, just beyond it, there was one. Not large, as I realized by fumbling round its edge, but not small. I didn't check if there was anything on the table. Such detail could come later. Besides, I would have knocked over any objects on the table, for sure.

I set out for the opposite wall, correctly expecting the table to be more or less in the middle of the room. I met no further obstacles till I reached the wall. I put out my hand to it and felt a painted surface that moved slightly with the pressure from my hand. I investigated the surface with both palms. It was panelled and it *did* move. Suddenly, I realized that I was standing at a door. A door! Great! It didn't take long to find the handle. It was a round knob. Holding my breath and hoping to open the door to a bright morning sun, I turned the knob and pushed. Nothing happened. I stepped aside and tried pulling. The door swung open easily (no horror-story creaks and groans, I'm afraid, and I can't offer you a dead body falling out of a cupboard either). But neither did I find any light. The antiseptic stench was much stronger in this room. Somehow I could sense that it was a small room, not much bigger than a cupboard. And indeed, it turned out to be the smallest room, as they say, in my new "home". My foot contacted a round drum and I leaned over it, feeling a loo seat at its top. It was one of those chemical toilets.

I left the loo and decided to return to the mattress by feeling my way round the wooden slatted walls. There had to be another door somewhere. After a couple of false alarms, I found it quite close to the bed. The door was just like the other one, it seemed, but with a handle rather than a knob. I pushed down on the handle and pulled, again bracing myself for the outside world. But nothing happened. I pushed instead. Nothing. I lifted up the handle and pushed and pulled. Still nothing. The door was locked and simply rattled. In fact, it rattled with the characteristic noise of a padlock on the other side. Doubly locked.

"Damn!" I plonked myself down on the mattress again. Remember that early Cure song, "Boys Don't Cry"? Yes, well, we just don't like to admit it, that's all. The foray into the room had sapped all of my courage and most of my strength (such as they were) so I lay down. In despair, I said to myself, "I should be out with Lisa today. We agreed on it. She'll think I've stood her up." This last thought filled me with horror. I almost blamed myself for letting her down. Sooner or later, though, depression gave way to tiredness and tedium. I dropped off to sleep again. What else was there to do?

Chapter 8

I woke to sounds. Shoes on floorboards. Loud and approaching the door near my bed. My initial reaction was relief. Normal sounds, familiar sounds. At last, something I recognized. But then, as the footsteps halted and keys were pushed first into the padlock and then into the keyhole in the door, alarm set in. Who was he? I was sure it was a "he". What had he come for? What would he do to me? I sat up but, I confess, I cowered on the mattress.

As the door began to open (inwards) a bit of light came into the room. It was much dimmer than direct daylight so I knew that the door didn't open directly to the great outdoors. There was a room beyond this one and, judging by the footsteps, it was not carpeted either. From behind the opening door the man uttered a surprised, "Oh." Then he stepped into the room and I caught sight of him in the diffuse beam of light coming through the door. His arms reached out over my head, there was a click and my eyes closed involuntarily against a sudden, bright light. While my eyes were recovering from the shock, I heard the man lock the door, this time from the inside. "Why on earth didn't you turn the light on?" he asked.

He was quite a tall chap, with a head of curly hair and a rather impish but nonetheless serious face. In his thirties, probably late thirties, I guessed. He was smart – jacket and tie. I looked at the floor and shrugged. "Didn't know it was there."

He shook his head. "This isn't the middle ages, you know. There's always a light switch." He looked down at me on the mattress and added, "If you were a cat, you'd lead a very safe life."

"What?"

"No curiosity. You've not even given the room the once-over for the light. Oh well, right now it's good for you not to be too curious. Should keep you alive." Before I could say anything, he changed the subject. "You haven't even had breakfast." He indicated the table.

I stood up and looked around. There was nothing at all sinister about the room any more. It was some sort of workmen's hut, I guessed. The table was laid for breakfast. Milk, cornflakes, sugar and so on. There was a sink and draining board along the wall that I had not fumbled along before. On top of a cupboard near the end of the mattress there was one of those electric fans that you see in all those sweaty, deep south American films. There was an easy chair too – rather the worse for wear but a comfy chair even so.

The man took the dining chair and sat down, his legs straddling either side of its back, facing me. "Now, young man. You may not be the most curious of characters but you'll have some questions for me. Let's get them out of the way, shall we?"

His forthright approach startled me. I hesitated before asking, "Where am I?"

"This," he replied, "is home. Everything here is yours. You'll be looked after."

"But where is this place?"

"I doubt if you'd expect me to answer fully all your questions."

I was too timid and unsure of myself to object to his response. Instead, I asked tamely, "What time is it?"

The man laughed. "The questions that you regard as trivial, and hence that I'll answer, happen to be the very ones that I think are really quite important. Far too delicate for me to answer. I wouldn't go to the bother of taking your watch and blacking out this room if I wanted you to know what time it is."

"But you've brought breakfast. It must be morning."

"Best way of disorientating people – bringing them inappropriate meals. Your next one might be supper." He smiled wryly but not unpleasantly.

"What day is it, then? Saturday?"

"Maybe. But," he said, "what about the big questions? 'Why am I here?' and so on."

I stood up and nervously walked over to the table. "I don't feel like breakfast," I said.

"Fair enough."

The man simply gazed at me in silence, content to let the nervous tension force a reaction from me. "Well," I said, "I'm not sure who you think I am, but I reckon you've got the wrong person."

"Nice try, Sebastian."

I hesitated but tried to continue the bluff. "Sebastian who?"

"Do you want me to recite your life history – and that of your family?" he replied. "Research is a wonderful thing."

"All right," I said, looking away from him. "Why am I here?"

He smiled. "Why do *you* think?"

I sighed. "You're blackmailing my father, I suppose."

"What?"

"You're . . ." I stopped. He had heard my reply in the first place so there was no need to repeat it and possibly make him more indignant than he already appeared to be.

"No," he said firmly. "This isn't blackmail."

I was, of course, dying to ask, "So what is it?" But I didn't. He didn't seem in the mood for it and I had no hope of getting a proper answer. "Oh," I muttered and sat down in the armchair. The man adjusted his seat to face me again but said nothing at all.

"What is this place?" I asked when I could no longer stand the quiet.

"A hut. A veritable palace compared to where you might have ended up."

"You don't give much away, do you?" I said.

The man shrugged. "I'm telling you as much as I can, to let you know where you stand. I don't want to add to your burden any more than I have to."

"If I start to yell when you're not here, won't someone hear me and come to rescue me?"

"Now that's more like a sensible question," he said. "But I'm afraid no one will hear. You're in a wilderness, of a sort, as far as the general public is concerned."

A wilderness, of a sort. What did that mean? Yet asking would do no good. He wouldn't answer. Instead, I plucked up the courage to look him directly in the face. "Who are you?" I asked.

"Mmm. You can call me ... let me see ... How about Frank?"

"Frank?"

"As in Bruno."

"It's not your real name."

He laughed. "Does MENSA know about you?" Then he added, with apparent sincerity, "Sorry, I don't mean to poke fun at you while you're still finding your feet. But anyway, there's no need for real names here."

"What are you going to do to me?"

Frank shrugged. "Nothing."

"Aren't you supposed to say, 'As long as you do what you're told,' at this point?"

"You've been watching too much television! I'm not going to tell you to do anything. You simply stay here. That's all. Think you can manage that?"

I looked around the room. "It's not going to be easy."

Frank smiled. "I'm here to take the sting out of it."

"How long will I be here?"

"Now, that I really don't know. It depends."

"On whether my dad cooperates?"

"How many times will I have to say it? This isn't blackmail, my young friend. You have a lot to learn."

"So, start to teach."

"Another time," he said, rising from the chair. "I must go. Is there anything you want — to make yourself more at home?"

"A get-away car."

Frank laughed. "That's better! Keep that up and we'll get along fine."

Chapter 9

After Frank had gone, I was sick with myself. I'd played the role of Mr Supercool, fraternizing with the enemy, instead of effecting a James Bond-style escape. Swift kick to the groin. Karate chop to the back of the neck of the doubled-up figure. Then, if necessary, a foot on the seat of his pants to propel him head-first into the wall. Grab the keys and Bob's your uncle. Freedom. Even if such stylish heroism was beyond me, I felt that at least I should have ranted and raved indignantly or simply hit him over the head with the breakfast bowl. But no, my sole resistance was in refusing to eat. I couldn't recall James Bond ever refusing to eat as a means of crushing the opposition.

Closer inspection of the table revealed that the

bowl-crashing-down-on-the-head tactic would have been useless anyway. It was a plastic bowl. The milk was in a carton too, not a bottle, and I was supplied only with a spoon – a plastic one at that. There was no knife in sight. Nothing that could even remotely resemble a weapon. It struck me though that, as Frank had said, it was time to explore. If there was something that might double as an offensive weapon, maybe it was still in a drawer.

I went first to the drawer in the sink unit. As I'd guessed, the remainder of the cutlery was stored in it. Plenty of knives and forks but again they were all plastic. The cupboard under the sink held more bowls, plates and cups – made from plastic, paper and polystyrene respectively. Even a polystyrene cup could be a weapon, I reasoned, if it was full of boiling water but, search as I might, I could not find a kettle. Clearly the room had been well and truly vetted. It crossed my mind then that I must have been dealing with professionals. The thought did not exactly cheer me. It meant that escape was unlikely.

My search of the room revealed the in-house entertainments, in the cupboard by the bed. Several jigsaw puzzles (which I hated), a game of Scrabble, a couple of packs of cards, a travelling chess set, some really classy literature (*Kane and Abel*, a Jackie Collins and two Harold Robbins), and a

Rubik's cube (remember them?). I knew then that I wasn't in for a whale of a time. No radio, no television, and no expensive hi-fi to remind me of home.

I took a seat on the not-so-comfy chair and thought. What was going on? If Frank was to be believed, it wasn't blackmail. If it wasn't blackmail, what was it? I couldn't believe that the whole kidnap ordeal had nothing to do with Dad's drugs business. I admit that I had no evidence that the two were connected but it was a massive coincidence if they weren't. Too much of a coincidence to credit it. I wondered if Frank would tell me. "Are you a drugs dealer, Frank?" Or "Is your favourite kind of bird a jackdaw?" No, more tact would be needed to elicit a response, or at least a non-violent one. After all, Frank had no reason to believe that I knew everything about Dad's underworld activities. If he was assuming my innocence and ignorance he'd be surprised, to put it mildly, at such a question. If he wasn't in that business, the question would simply get Dad into hotter water by admitting, in effect, the Flude household's involvement. No, I'd have to be diplomatic about it.

My stomach let out a mighty rumbling, reminding me of the foolishness of refusing to eat the enemy's food. So I swallowed my pride and, soon after, the cornflakes too. One advantage of cornflakes was the crunching noise. Seriously. One of the worst things about my imprisonment was the utter silence of the prison. Any relief from that deathly quiet was welcome: the crunching of cereals, talking to myself, tapping a foot on the wooden floor, anything. If I was going to crack under the pressure of the kidnap, I thought then that it would be the silence that got to me. The only sound of a life apart, the fragile rhythm of my heart. Fifteen years of living with a musician had not exactly equipped me for coping with silence. Pete Flude was to peace and quiet what Chernobyl was to the environment. I resolved to ask Frank for a radio or something.

"Well," I said to myself. "This ain't gonna be a bundle of laughs." I turned to the "games cupboard".

Frank's return interrupted the fifth game of patience (one success, three failures, and the fifth doomed to failure). "That's more like it," he said, locking the door with one hand and carrying a coffee pot in the other. "I see you're settling in nicely."

"Hardly."

"Okay, but you're coping. That's good enough. Anyway," he added brightly, "want a coffee?"

I nodded. Deciding to test my theory about the lack of kettle straightaway, I said, "I could have murdered one straight after breakfast."

"I couldn't supply one then," Frank said. "Get the mugs out."

"I'm sorry. My hospitality doesn't stretch to real mugs. Just grotty polystyrene things."

"They'll do."

He didn't rise to that bait either so I asked, "Why didn't you leave me with a kettle so I could brew my own?"

Frank laughed. "Because I don't fancy a mugful of scorching water over me as I come in, that's why."

"How do you mean?"

"Don't act so innocent, young man. Only a fool would not have hatched a few plots by now. You might as well ask me for a sawn-off shotgun."

I was going to admit good humouredly to my weapon search but remembering that I didn't want to be appeased by Frank's niceties, I changed the subject and asked sullenly, "Why do you want to keep me in the dark regarding the time of day?"

"Disorientation."

"So you said. Why disorientate me?"

"It makes people . . . mm . . . placid. Less likely to try anything silly. Anyway," he said, "you're not turning militant on me, are you?"

"Why not? You turned militant on me."

"Your militancy would be pointless. Ours wasn't. It brought you here."

I was learning quickly that, throughout the

coming weeks, Frank was always going to be one step ahead of me. Impossible to argue against. At the same time, he was so cool and pleasant. I never knew whether to like him or hate him. In any other situation, he might be a good friend. In the workman's hut, he was the enemy. And an apparently friendly enemy seemed to me to be the worst type. The occasional beating would have been less disorientating than his pleasantries. But I guess that I've put my finger on it: it was all part of his silly disorientation process. Anyway, Frank was on the topic of my abduction so I decided to try to capitalize on it.

"Why *am* I here? You say it's not blackmail but I bet it's something to do with Dad." Frank's shrug neither denied nor confirmed it, so I decided to push my luck further. "What is it about Dad that's caused all this?"

"Not bad coffee, eh? None of your instant muck."

"You're not Customs and Excise, are you, punishing him for illegally importing bad quality instant coffee?"

That got a reaction from Frank. Not prolonged or obvious, but a reaction all the same. If it wasn't such a stupid saying, I'd have to say that his brow knitted – just for a moment. Anyway, I took it to mean that I'd struck a chord, that I was barking up the *right* tree.

"I've got time for a game of Scrabble," Frank said, "if you want one."

Yes, I thought. I could put down "drugs" or "crack" and see how he reacted to that. But in the event I decided against. I'd gone as far as I dared for one day. I sipped the coffee instead of answering him. "Mm. It's good. Where did you make it?"

He jerked his thumb in the direction of the door. "There's a room outside."

"Do you sleep there or will I be on my own?"

"That would be telling."

I grimaced. "Don't you think that what you're doing is . . . rather unchristian?"

"I'd rather be rich than righteous or holy."

It was my turn to react. "That's a misquote from The Smiths!" I blurted out.

Frank shrugged and denied it. "The Smiths? Never heard of them."

Whatever was going on, Frank was getting paid for kidnapping me. And I was sure that I'd found that he was acquainted with that Smiths song. I decided to quote some more to goad him. " 'This position I have, It pays my way, But it corrodes my soul'." (And, yes, Dad did use the same quotation a few chapters back.)

"The Smiths, eh?" Frank said. "Sound interesting."

"All right," I said. "What about this game of Scrabble?"

Okay, so I fraternized with the enemy. But don't judge me too harshly. I did it because he was there. Because he was another human being. Without him there was nothing but solitude and silence.

After the game (which I won – clearly Scrabble wasn't one of Frank's strengths) I was feeling peckish. "What's for dinner, or lunch or tea?" I asked.

"Sandwiches, I should think," Frank replied.

"Good job you're not feeding me on beef steak."

"Why not?" he asked.

"The plastic knives would never get through it."

"Good point. We'll fatten you up on gateau instead."

"Ugh."

"No? Most people would jump at the chance of living on Black Forest for a while."

"I'm looking after my figure," I replied.

"You're not a health food freak, are you? If God had meant us to eat health food, He wouldn't have given us taste buds."

I had to smile, even at an enemy. "Not health food exactly," I said. "Just good food."

"Okay," he answered, "I'll bear it in mind. Anything else, while we're at it?"

"I'll need some fresh clothes some time soon."

"Mm, that's a bit awkward. I'm not going to be seen buying clothes that don't fit me. Bad publicity! Strip off," he said, "and wash what you've got on.

They won't take long to dry in here. Gets fairly hot. You can wash yourself while you're at it. No bath, I'm afraid."

"Great," I said, less than enthusiastically. "There's another thing too."

"What's that?"

"I'd like a radio. To break the silence."

Frank shook his head. "No radios. But I'll see what I can do. Maybe a Walkman, with a few Afterglow tapes, eh?"

"Anything," I said. "Even Afterglow."

"Is that it?" said Frank, rising from his chair, "or is there anything else you want?"

"Some paper would help. Plain paper and pencils. I like to sketch things."

"I think not. I don't want you keeping a diary – or sketching me if it comes to that."

"Well, how about books? Your library's a bit duff. Will you get me some decent books?"

"Decent? What? Shakespeare?"

"Not that decent. Some Graham Greene or something. Oh, there's a few set books I ought to have to carry on . . ."

"I've nothing against Graham Greene," Frank interrupted, "but no school books. Rather a give-away don't you think, for me to go and buy such things? How about a razor? Have you started shaving yet?" Seeing me shake my head, he added, "Anything else?"

"Well," I replied, "to quote that Smiths' song again, 'I want to leave, You will not miss me'."

Frank grunted. As he unlocked the door, he replied, "You're a flatulent pain in the arse. That's what you are." He grinned as he closed the door behind him.

Looking back, it seems such a trivial little triumph. By quoting the last line of the song, Frank had, under my pressure, admitted to knowing it. "So what?" you might be thinking. Let me assure you that any victory, however minor, was quite a consolation in those circumstances. Not for itself but because it gave me hope. I came out on top that time; maybe I could come out on top again. Anyway, proving his knowledge of the song turned out not to be as trivial as you might think it now and as I thought it at the time.

Chapter 10

Let's skip a few days. Besides, one day was much the same as any other in Frank's Hotel, and I could not tell one from another. I thought, though, that I was more or less keeping track of the days because, as Frank had said, it did get very hot in the room: I assumed that it was about mid-day every time the heat was almost unbearable and the electric fan was essential to human survival.

About ten days into the kidnap, I estimated, and Frank was still making his frequent visits as chef, waiter, companion and tormentor. His schedule, as far as I could make out, was totally erratic. Presumably, this was designed both to help and to hinder. Not settling into a routine meant that I was not as bored as I might have been. On the other hand, irregularity also disorientated. I was sure that his ploy was working – I *had* become placid. Thoughts of escape did not exactly come thick and fast. The futility of contemplating escape, on the other hand, haunted me frequently. I had also become established in the room. I had a cassette player, albeit a cheap one that could make a double bass sound tinny, a few good books, and I had already started carving my name on the inside panel of one of the cupboards. Having only plastic tools, I knew that it was going to take time so I started early. I'm not totally sure why I did it, really. I wanted to leave behind me an impression on the room and a clue. Perhaps rubbing away with a plastic knife gave more purpose to my time in the hut. Perhaps it was a substitute for a realistic plan of escape.

To say that each minute, each hour, each day, was dull is quite an understatement. I'll tell you how bad it was: I even did a couple of jigsaws. That's real boredom for you, when jigsaws come as welcome relief! There's also a limit to the buzz you can get from games of patience and ten dodgy tapes. I did have plenty to think about, though. Since Dad was so important to the Drugs Squad, I assumed that legions of their best men would be working on my case. This thought was quite comforting even though there was no sign of the cavalry charging over the hill. I also wondered about Mum and Dad, and Lisa. Mum would have withdrawn into herself. She wouldn't be voicing her fears for me, she'd simply be absorbing them, crucifying herself. If Dad had any gigs, he'd still do them. He wouldn't want to let anyone down. They'd be magnificent performances too. He'd stomp around the stage like an angry giant. He'd work the passion out of his body up there in front of everyone. And the performance would only be ended when he had nothing left. By the time he got home, he'd be drained, like a zombie. If there were no gigs, he'd work it out of his system in the studio instead. I guessed that there would probably be a wonderful crop of new and very angry songs in the Flude repertoire. Dad always expressed himself best and freely in song. And what about Lisa? If I weren't cooped up, what might we be doing together? I haunted myself with imagined possibilities. I cared for her so much, but she could have been believing that I was avoiding her. You see, I had no guarantee that the police would come clean about my predicament. Given the sensitivity of the case and Dad's role, they could have been keeping quiet about it. My beaming face might not have been transmitted every night on *News at Ten*, and I doubt if *Crimewatch* would feature me for the same reason. But enough of my dreary thoughts, let's get back to some action.

I skipped to this particular day because it marked

a new relationship with Frank. I had been probing gently for the cause of my kidnap and not getting that far. Frank's reactions like that resulting from the smuggled coffee jibe wouldn't stand up in a court of law, but my intuition was convinced. I decided to go in search of scientific proof. I had learned that Frank was far more touchy about everyday things (the time and date, for example) than he was about the larger issues. So I'd decided to tackle him head-on about Dad and drug dealing. If I was right about Frank, he might just talk about it. Why not? I was hardly in a position to endanger any of his illicit operations.

Frank entered with a tray, put it down and immediately, as always, went through the door-locking routine. The tray contained two main courses, apparently sausages and other, unidentifiable things swimming in a gory red sauce, all kept in place by a ring of brown rice. "Grub up," he chimed.

Sometimes Frank ate with me, sometimes he simply watched. This day he was sociable. That suited me because we could talk over the meal. After the first few forkfuls and the initial shock of the spices, the sausage dish turned out to be very nice, despite appearances. "I don't know what this is exactly, but it's okay. Lots of tasty E numbers."

"You've got something on your mind."

"Yes, well. Hostages don't have much to do but think, you know."

"So what's the burning issue?"

"Me. Dad. Drugs. That sort of thing." I couldn't bring myself to look at him as I delivered my thunderbolt so I don't know if a frown flickered, a smile slithered or astonishment strayed across his face.

"You, Pete Flude, and drugs? What do you mean?"

"I mean, why am I here? It's connected with my dad and drugs, isn't it?" At the end of the question, I did look at him. He was nodding slowly. Not, I thought, to answer affirmatively but simply to acknowledge that an anticipated question had actually and finally been asked.

"So he told you about that?"

"We're an open and honest lot, us Fludes."

"How open and honest?"

"Very open and honest," I replied.

"I see. But you thought that I was blackmailing your father."

"Not for money. To continue as a courier."

"Ah, I see," Frank responded, giving nothing further away.

"Well?"

"Well? You seem to expect an answer but you haven't asked me anything."

Perhaps he was getting just a little niggled. "Is the object of this exercise," I said, indicating the room and my encapsulation within it, "to force

Dad to act as courier?"

"I've said several times that your dad isn't being blackmailed – so I can't now say that he is. You'll have to think it out for yourself."

It struck me from his tone that he now regretted his earlier denials that he was involved in blackmail. For the sake of an easy life, he would have preferred simply to confirm my theory and have done with it. He was probably annoyed with himself more than with me.

"Is that all you're going to say? 'Think it out for yourself'?"

"No. I'll tell you the ingredients of the meal if you want."

"No," I said. "It doesn't matter. I've no great use for recipes in here."

After he'd gone, I did think it out for myself. It dawned on me suddenly really. It turned out to be fairly obvious. Perhaps you're way ahead of me, having worked it out for yourselves. If so, you can feel pleased with yourselves and skip a paragraph. If not, start by considering the events leading to the unfortunate shooting of the Jackdaw by the Drugs Squad. Dad had said that the police had been able to put a tail (that's the correct technical term, if you believe what you hear on the box) on the Jackdaw after Dad's second contact with the mob. He also said that the Jackdaw slipped his tail. That implied that the Jackdaw knew the police were on to him in the first place. Clearly, the Jackdaw's boss would wonder why one of his men – and a clever one by all accounts – was being tailed. Surely, he'd suspect a leak – a police mole in his ranks (more technical jargon with which I'll assume that you're familiar). Then came the shooting – some time after the African job in which the new recruit was one Pete Flude. It all added up to Mr Big suspecting Dad of police collaboration. Maybe the African exercise was not even a real job at all but an invention to test Dad's faithfulness. If so, he'd failed the test.

So, if Dad's "understanding" with the Drugs Squad was known, why had I been kidnapped? This was the worst thought of all, because it could be little else but pure retribution. Frank had told the truth: there was no need or use for blackmail if Dad's cover was well and truly blown. The only logical necessity was for punishment. And using the principle that the young and innocent spectator makes a more effective victim than the original sinner himself, I was chosen for special treatment. (When Miss Greene read this part, she launched into Latin. Luckily, she also translated the quotation. "Though guiltless, you must pay the penalty for your father's sins." Quite apt really.) Whilst I still reserved a thought for what Mum and Dad were going through – especially Dad who would consider himself responsible for my predicament –

I must confess that at that time I worried more about how far the punishment would go. Just how ruthless were Frank and the Jackdaw's mob? I shuddered and tried to banish the thought from my brain.

I waited for Frank's next visit, half expecting to see him with a 12-bore shotgun, whips, a chainsaw or something. But nothing like it. He entered with a grin and a happy greeting. "Good news!"

"What?" I asked suspiciously. Did he mean it? Was I to get new clothes, some decent tapes? Or was I free to go? Good news seemed remote then – and unattainable.

"'The Best Years' is at number one," Frank replied. "The bad news is that it won't be there for long. Madonna's just released another single."

I wasn't really in the mood for banter. I was still stricken from my discovery that anything might happen to me during the punishment. "Don't celebrate the success of the man you're trying to punish," I replied.

"Punish?"

"Yes. It isn't blackmail. It's retribution."

"Ah," he said, "you've taken my advice and figured it out for yourself."

"Am I right?"

"Of course."

So there we have it – the power of logic and

deduction. But where to now? How would my knowledge affect me, and my relationship with Frank? Would it help or hinder? In fact, it had a startling effect on Frank. He became quite talkative and open about the whole affair. I guess that he realized that there was no longer any point to great secrecy. By being . . . well . . . frank about it, he wasn't telling me anything that I didn't already know anyway. He simply filled in a few holes and told the same story from the opposite viewpoint. And, of course, I was in no position to do anything with my knowledge. The following conversation actually took place over two or three visits but I'll report it as if it had been continuous – for the sake of coherence.

"So you're," I asked rather naively but really to initiate our man-to-man chat, "what's known as a drugs baron?"

Frank laughed. "Hardly. Barons are powerful and rich. I'm not that."

"And what about the Jackdaw? Was he powerful and rich?"

"Who?"

"The Jackdaw. That's what the police called him at any rate. The chap who got shot."

"Oh, we didn't know they called him that. Very . . . er . . . imaginative. I reckon they employ someone full time to invent codenames for villains and operations. Still, it's just harmless police routine,"

Frank said in an almost mocking tone.

"You sound sceptical of police routine."

Frank smiled. "The police have their strengths, I guess. They think of their methodical routine as a strength, no doubt. But we see it as a weakness to be exploited. Routine methods are by nature predictable. And it's useful to be able to predict the behaviour of an adversary. Very useful."

"So," I said, "you're confident about winning the . . . er . . . drugs war, or whatever the newspapers call it."

"War," Frank pondered. "Not a bad word for it, at the moment."

"Why at the moment?" Then I twigged. "Ah, the battle over crack, you mean?"

Frank was taken aback a little. I still had some ability to surprise him. "You *are* well informed, young man."

"Made in Bolivia, processed in Columbia. Then into America and, if you have your way, into Britain."

"All right," Frank said, "I don't need a geography lesson."

"Yes. I'm sorry. I was just showing off, I suppose."

"Yes. But you're not far wide of the mark. Everyone's getting polarized on the issue of crack. There *is* a war over it."

"Between who?" I asked.

"The police, hell bent on keeping it out of Britain, and people like – what was it? – the Jackdaw, determined to get it in. You see," he said, "it's not big business, it's enormous business. And people tend to be very . . . protective of their business when fortunes are at stake." He thought for a moment then continued, "The police seem to be going for a big kill in order to deter dealers. To do so, they're using dirty tricks – like involving your father. Then we're forced to play dirtier tricks – like kidnapping. Both sides are taking up extreme but opposite positions. Heavy tactics. Interesting times we live in."

"How much dirtier is it going to get, Frank?"

"That's not up to me," he replied.

It was clear that he wasn't going to say any more. Perhaps the answer was too ominous to contemplate anyway, so I changed tack. "When you come down to it, crack's such big business because it's so addictive, isn't it?" I asked.

Frank nodded. "Captive market," he said.

"Don't you find it just a bit difficult to sleep at night? An awful lot of lives are being ruined."

"There are worse businesses to be in," Frank replied as if he'd justified it to himself on many occasions. "Bar tenders and brewers sleep well at night but alcohol is a far bigger killer. Then there's car manufacturers and tobacconists – they're mass murderers in comparison. It's not the products and dealers that are the problem. It's the people that abuse the products. Only fools get hooked on alcohol – or crack."

I decided not to continue to criticize his chosen career and instead went back to his comment about the dirty trick of kidnapping. At least, I think I did. Hopefully you'll forgive me and understand if I don't get the order of things perfectly precise. "You say that kidnapping me was a very dirty trick, but what's it for, exactly?"

"You already know. You told me."

"Yes, but what purpose does punishment serve?"

"It's a . . . warning, if you like," Frank answered.

I didn't really follow. "Warning?"

"A warning to people like your father."

"Oh, I see," I said. "Double-cross us in our efforts to introduce crack here and your nearest and dearest will pay." Frank merely shrugged but I must have been right. It made sense that, to establish crack here, suppliers would have to be seen to be dealing harshly with those who tried to thwart them. Rather than ask again about the implications for me of this harsh treatment – the answer was unlikely to be forthcoming anyway – I continued with the logic and deduction. "That's why you're willing to talk about all this, isn't it?" I said. "It's effective as a warning only if it's known why Pete Flude's being punished! You hope that when it's all over, I'll sell my story to the press or whatever and then everyone will know the fate awaiting double-crossers."

"You do think of yourself as perceptive today."

"Bet I'm right, though," I ventured. I suppose that I should have been relieved that Frank needed to keep me alive if I was to tell the tale. But I didn't dwell on the thought at the time. I was hungry for more divulgences. "I do wonder why you take on the likes of Dad if they're so . . . unreliable."

I remember Frank's reply to this very clearly. Probably because it sounded so clever. "The organized criminal seeks two victims," he said. "The first – the primary victim – is the victim of the crime itself. The person robbed, mugged, sold dope, or whatever. The second victim is the innocent person who takes the rap for the crime if anything goes wrong. Bad criminals forget the secondary victim and usually take that role themselves. To satisfy the tidy mind of the policeman and get him off your back, there's nothing like a secondary victim. Well," Frank cleared his throat, "your dad was originally conceived of as a secondary victim. Born and bred for it. If it went wrong, he'd get done for smuggling. But we made a mistake." He gave one of his wry smiles. "We knew he used grass but we didn't know he was under surveillance because of it. But we now surmise that he must have been and did a deal with the drugs squad. Correct?" Frank had nearly got it right, but apparently he didn't know that their American operation had been infiltrated. I didn't want to say anything in case I put my foot in it. I used Frank's own favourite trick of simply shrugging. He took it as confirmation of his version of events and said, "The best laid plans . . ."

"Do you often . . . use rock stars?"

"Use them? As couriers, you mean?" I nodded. "It's not unheard of," Frank replied. "They tour around a lot, often to convenient locations. And they carry lots of equipment in which all manner of things can be concealed. But it's not like it was a good few years back. These days many of them are too moral and incorruptible to touch drugs. They may not look as pious as Cliff Richard but . . ." He smiled to himself but did not say any more.

"This punishment, Frank," I asked. "Why me? Why didn't you go straight for Dad?"

"Don't fall into the trap of thinking the police are fools. They can add two and two when they need to. Just like you did. They knew they'd blown it and their man was at risk. It would have been easier to get at the Queen than Pete Flude, especially at home. You probably didn't notice that your place was like Fort Knox. They did a tidy job. We went for you instead. It has some advantages."

"They protected Dad but not me?" I felt piqued and dejected.

"Don't underestimate yourself – or the police.

You had protection that night but we . . . waylaid it."

"Waylaid? You mean . . ." My mind raced back to the car crash that I'd witnessed from the back of the bus.

"Your minders' unmarked car got marked, involved in a little accident."

I guessed that I hadn't helped my minders either. That night, I left the gig unexpectedly early, I didn't go on to Lisa's place afterwards. Generally, I'd acted unpredictably.

I remember the enlightening conversation with Frank finishing with more comments about my role in his feud with the Fludes. "I can see that, in your terms, I'm the primary victim of your kidnapping but," I asked, "who's the secondary victim for it?"

Frank got out of the easy chair and prepared to leave as he answered. "That's where you and I have something in common," he said. "I'm a victim too – the secondary one."

"But you're hardly what I'd describe as an innocent party," I objected.

"No," he replied. "That's true. But as I said when you asked if I was a drugs baron, I'm just a little fish in a big sea. I'm expendable. None of the big fish will come near here. If it goes wrong . . . well, that's what they pay me for. Anyway," he added, "time I was elsewhere. You okay?"

"Well, there's something I've been meaning to ask you for."

"Oh, yes?"

"I'd like a guitar – acoustic, that is."

"Yeah? Any good, are you?" He seemed genuinely interested.

"I know one string from another. That's about it."

"Okay, that's enough. I'll get you one. We can have a few choruses of 'She'll Be Comin' Round the Mountain'."

"I don't know that one," I said. "Is it the new Madonna single?"

"No," he said as he opened the door. "It's much too sophisticated for Madonna."

Chapter 11

I got my guitar. I played quite a lot. As another means of breaking the dreadful silence of that hut, it soothed me enormously. Whenever I felt tension and depression coming on, the guitar helped to relax me. I even played a little for Frank. He really seemed to appreciate it too. But our harmonious relationship did not last for long. The worst chapter in my story so far is about to unfold. Here beginneth the aforementioned destruction of a schoolboy.

It was a good few hours after the hottest part of the day, so my guess was that it was evening, when the first and only noises from the outside world drifted into my prison. It was a bark. A dog's bark. A bark like a fog horn. The noise took me by surprise. I didn't stop to think. I simply froze, listened for a moment, heard it again, and then shouted, "GB?" Nothing. Silence. Maybe there were a couple of voices. I couldn't be sure. I shouted again. "GBH! Is that you?" Definitely nothing this time. Normality had returned to my silent prison.

The whole episode lasted for less than thirty seconds, I suppose but its repercussions lasted a whole lot longer. Why didn't I stop to think before I opened my big mouth?

I was convinced that I'd heard Lisa's Rottweiler. Totally convinced by its characteristic bark. You'll probably be thinking, "One dog sounds much like another. It could have been any big dog." But I'd reply, "You haven't heard GB!"

It took several minutes after my shouting for me to realize the extreme folly of my action. If GB had been there, someone would be with him, no doubt. Lisa and/or her parents. I suppose that I'd been so pleased to hear something from the outside world that I'd been fooled into believing that it would be something pleasant. GB and Lisa leading the cavalry charge. But how could they have known that I was there in the hut? Ruling out incredible coincidences, they would only be there if they knew I was being held in it; that is, if they were connected in some way with my kidnap. And if they were involved then, by shouting out GB's name, I'd just told them that I'd made the connection between my kidnap, the Woodwards and hence the whole drugs business. The result: I'd put myself in even greater danger than I was before the GB incident.

Clearly, though, Lisa herself was no drugs baron. It had to be someone else in her family. Her father presumably. If, as Frank had indicated, the big fish wouldn't come near the site of my kidnap in case of incrimination, then perhaps it was Lisa with GB. Or perhaps Mr Woodward wasn't a big fish at all. No, I ruled that out. I'd been to his rather luxurious house. For a scrap metal dealer, he was doing very well indeed. Suddenly, I felt sure that he was the man that the police were after – the Jackdaw's boss.

Then the floodgates opened. That sullen evening with Lisa. It made sense. She'd set me up! She'd delivered me to a specific place at a specific time. The grumpiness was feigned to get me away from the club and on to the appropriate bus. Perhaps throughout our "affair" she'd been encouraged by her father. A link to poor innocent Seb Flude would have been most useful to him – in case dear old Pete Flude turned out to be unreliable. On top of that, the police were bound to have interviewed her because she was the last person to see me in my unkidnapped state, so she'd have had the opportunity to shop her dad as the Crack and

Kidnap King of Totley Brook. Obviously she valued him more than me in her life. With every thought, I became more convinced of Woodward's involvement and guilt. With every thought, the screw turned a little tighter and my torment increased. I'd been wrong ever to think that Lisa might be associating with me to get to Dad. All along she'd been after me all right, but not in the way I'd hoped for and imagined. Perhaps she'd never cared for me at all. That last thought really hurt – more than all the rest put together.

My only consolations at that time were weak and overwhelmed by the torments. But I held on to three crumbs of comfort. If it was Lisa outside, why was she there? Had she come to help me? I wished that I could be convinced that she had. Secondly, she had been *very* grumpy on the night of the kidnap. Perhaps she was acting on her father's orders against her will and didn't like it at all. In other words, Lisa's dad could have been using *her* to get to Pete Flude. Via me, of course. Just possibly, she was an unwitting bridge to me and our relationship *was* of her own volition. Maybe she had felt something for me after all, but it was hard to clutch at this straw in the light of her setting me up as she had done.

Finally, I came to realize that I actually approved of Dad's collaborating with the police. He had made a stand against something that he disliked.

Okay, it had landed me in it, but I wouldn't have had it any other way. Frank and Woodward's business seemed loathsome to me. It had to be fought even if I became a victim of the war. This third crumb of comfort was quite important to me. It meant that no matter how badly it went for me something positive could be salvaged from it.

Frank's next appearance was much delayed. I had been to sleep twice, worked out two guitar riffs which were pleasant and possibly original, tried to put lyrics to them but ended up in the "I'll be your anchor in stormy seas" school of writing, and played many games and cassettes before his overdue visit. I greeted him with, "Good day. What kept you?" but most unusually for Frank, he said nothing at all as he came in. Even odder, he didn't lock the door. He threw onto the table a holdall that he was carrying. He still didn't reply as he placed the kitchen chair in the middle of the room, facing away from the door. Then, at last, he spoke. "Come and sit here, please."

I was so dumbfounded by his formality and request-cum-order that I got up from the armchair and obeyed. It was only when I was virtually on the chair that I asked, "Why?"

Avoiding looking at me, he said, "You'll find out."

Quick as a flash, he produced some rope from his bag and I'd hardly spluttered out, "What's going on?" before my legs were bound to the chair.

"Certain decisions have been made," Frank said as he grasped both my wrists in one of his big hands and drew a rope tight about them with the other, "regarding your future. Please don't struggle. I don't wish to hurt you." He stood in front of me and held my head in both his hands so I could look neither to right nor left. Then he shouted over my head, "Come in!"

The door opened and someone else, a man I thought, came in. While Frank held me so I could do nothing but look straight ahead at his chest, the second man bound my trunk to the back of the chair. Out of the corner of my eye I could just make out the sleeves of his blue shirt as his arms coiled the rope around my body. My arms were left unbound but my hands were still tied together.

Frank stepped back, satisfied that the job was done. It was all so fast and efficient that I hardly had a chance to protest. By the time that I'd recovered from the shock and intimidation of being constrained and was ready to fight against it, it was all over. Very professional. Ten out of ten for style, team-work and taking the enemy by surprise.

"What. . .?" I didn't say any more because the man behind me was already springing the next surprise. A blindfold was thrown over my eyes and tied at the back of my head. "What's this for?" I cried.

"I would have thought it rather obvious, Seb,"

Frank said. "You've seen me, you know me. But you don't need to see anyone else. My . . . colleague here has to prepare something for you and administer it. He prefers not to be seen while he's doing it."

"What?" I asked. Actually, I blurted. "What do you mean?"

The other man said coolly, "We'll kick off with 250 milligrammes."

It was Frank's turn to sound indignant. "What?" he said. "He's only a kid, remember."

"Okay," the second man conceded. "I'll make it 150 and take it from there."

"What's going on?" In my private blackness, I could only hear and feel. I felt a tight band around my upper left arm. Then a dab of something cold – ether – on the lower arm. Having already cried out and blurted, it was time for screaming. "No!"

As I felt the prick in my arm, my mouth was shouting. "Why? Why?" But my brain was thinking, Because I know too much. And they know it. Frank must have heard me calling to GB. Mr Big is the scrap metal dealer from Totley Brook with the big posh house, pots of money, the pleasant wife and the gorgeous treacherous daughter. Treacherous to me, of course, not to her father.

After the injection, I felt an immediate period of tranquillity, like effortlessly floating in calm water. I don't know if it was the instant effect of whatever

I'd been doped with, or simply the fatalistic calm of knowing that it had been injected and there was nothing I could do but accept its presence in my body.

In that peaceful period of calm, I retained my powers of reasoning. In fact, everything was absolutely clear to me. They were trying to destroy my mind – maybe the body too. But the objective was to erase from my mind all memory of GB's bark. And, of course, all that the bark implied. Also, I reasoned, if I'd been given a hallucinatory drug – which I was soon to learn that I had – it seemed a likely and appropriate punishment for the Fludes. To mess up the son with heroin, LSD or whatever. I know that it will sound crazy but in that carefree state of meditation I accepted that form of punishment as both legitimate and inevitable.

Let me take a break at this point to make a couple of observations. Besides, I need a breather. The last few pages have been very difficut for me to write. First observation: if I appeared to endure the tying up, blindfolding and injecting rather stoically or with stiff upper lip, it's just that my true (scared witless) state got lost in poetic licence. The reported cries of "Oh, no. Please don't do that, sir," are simply a translation of whatever I actually said. The fact is that I can't remember very well but I'm sure that I betrayed far more cowardice and indulged in more terrified raving than this account suggests.

Second general observation: the days, weeks or whatever it was that followed the first injection were awful. It wasn't long before I couldn't distinguish reality from fantasy. So I'm going to write exactly what I thought was happening. Much of it may sound like nonsense, I suppose, because it couldn't possibly have happened under my circumstances at the time. But the point is that *I* thought it *was* happening. To me it was all real.

Back to my floating state. No anxieties at all. I knew that I was being punished and my mind was under assault but I didn't worry about it. I had my head in the clouds, you might say. In fact I was standing high on a hillside just below the clouds. I knew exactly where I was: a favourite spot in the Pennines. I remember most the freshness of the air, the absolute stillness and the vivid colours. The layer of cloud above me was pure white, the sky turquoise and the sun a bright gold. I found that I could look directly at the sun without hurting my eyes. Below me, the valley was lush and green, sliced in two by the perfectly straight railway line. There was a hamlet which, at a distance, looked like an idyllic toy village. Nothing moved, reinforcing the notion that the whole scene was a model and not the real thing at all. Beside me there was only a grey rock, where a few weeks ago there had stood both the rock and Lisa.

I felt that Lisa could and should be there somewhere, out of sight. Maybe in the village, or on a train that at any moment might hurry through the valley on its way to or from Sheffield. Something inside urged me to go down into the valley where I might find her. There was no obvious path but the slope was not particularly steep so I headed straight down. The descent was not too arduous at first and the differing heights afforded ever-changing views of the valley. Before long, though, I reached a steep section where the ground was stony. Walking down on this surface was unpleasant and difficult. The sharp downward slope made my knees and the backs of my legs ache, and there was the constant danger of slipping and sliding.

Suddenly anxiety had returned: the worry of losing my footing, and the worsening of the pain in my legs. I stopped walking for a while and looked around. The colours had faded from bright to pastel with the exception of the sun which was now yellow and harsh. I felt hot and sweaty. Yet something inside still made me carry on down the hillside. I put out a foot on to a large stone, only to have it roll away from me. I fell on to my back and my head hit something solid and blunt. My body started to tumble but I couldn't do anything about it. My mind had been dazed by the blow. I knew only that I was clattering downwards, painfully. Eventually I did come to a stop. On a softer surface. I must have rolled all the way down to where the rocks gave way to grass. I didn't try to get to my feet.

No, not grass. I was lying on the mattress, feeling bruised and battered. I was neither tied nor blindfolded. A voice, Frank's, said, "Back with us?" At first I couldn't see him in the room. In the centre of my vision there was a hazy circle as if the ferocious sun had burnt its negative imprint into my eye. "Here," he said, walking through the blue mist. "Eat this." He handed me something and I ate it. Whatever it was, it was minty and sweet. Presumably it was an energy-rich food, designed to sustain.

After recovering for a while on the mattress, I stumbled across the room, ignoring Frank altogether, and went to the toilet. I wished that it had a bolt on the inside. I could have sat in there, safely locked away from the next dose. But there was no lock, no safe harbour from Frank and his colleague. When I emerged, I asked, "How long?"

Frank seemed to understand me. He looked at his watch and answered, "He'll be here in half an hour." Thirty minutes of sanity then an unknown period of oblivion. "Drink?" he asked.

I expected tea or coffee but the polystyrene cup contained something cold, sharp and fruity. Some weird cocktail of fruit juices. After I'd finished it, I sat cross-legged on the bed and played guitar for a while. I probably sang a bit too. I don't know.

Frank seemed content to sit in silence and watch me. I hoped that he was feeling too bad, too guilty about his actions to dare to say anything to me. Perhaps he was just being professional – not getting involved. Or maybe he knew that I wouldn't want to speak to him after his unspeakable treatment of me. I didn't care then about his motives for silence but I appreciated it, content to ignore his presence. You see, I was too numbed by it all to complain or resist. I was too depressed even to be angry.

My mind was drifting, miles away, when the light went out and the door opened. I do remember that I was blindfolded again but I think I was simply held down on the mattress rather than tied to a chair when the next dose was administered. This time, though, my body reacted differently. I didn't suddenly drift off on a sea of tranquillity with all burdens lifted from my shoulders. For a while I remained in this world, my senses acute. More acute than before the injection. In fact, a first bit of fighting spirit seemed to have been injected into my veins. A sudden thought of escape struck me. The man with the syringe had just come through the door. Perhaps he hadn't locked it. When Frank's weight eventually ceased to hold me down, I jumped up and made a dash for the door. I was so familiar with every centimetre of that room that even blindfolded I knew exactly where the door was. But I didn't stop to ponder how it opened, where the handle was or anything like that. I just ran at it, apparently expecting my weight to jolt it open. I hit it with a thud. I felt the door shudder under my impact before I slithered to the floor.

There were voices in the room. "That shouldn't happen yet!" This voice was angry. "Are you sure," it continued, "that was only 200 milligrammes?"

There was a reply but I didn't catch it. Besides, by then I wasn't that bothered. One hundred, two hundred or three, what's the difference? There were other voices in my ears too. It was Lisa. I couldn't see her, or anything else, but I heard her. "That's lovely. I thought you said that you were hopeless." I listened intently in case another coherent sentence rose above the general hubbub. I picked out a male voice. "Want to hear another?" it asked. "Oh yes!" she replied eagerly. I gave her a quick burst.

> *Breaking free*
> *from earthly skin*
> *you cast aside the shell*
> *and dry yourself*
> *then fly on silver wings*
>
> *Dragonfly*
> *you dive and roll*
> *Glittering prize to me*
> *Your colours shine*
> *and fill my joyless soul*

Fly to me
Dazzle and dive
then hover here a while
On gauzy wings
we could live, gauzy lives

Please don't go
Slender body
beauty that can't be bound
Dragonfly girl
you dart away from me.

As I sang, I could see her, but only in semi-darkness. She was little more than an outline. When I'd finished, her head nodded approval. Her lips said, "Okay, it's your dad's song, but you *can* put heart and soul into it." I smiled. I wanted to reply but she'd gone. Fluttered away. I could not – would not – clip those wings.

The image of Lisa was dark but welcome. You might wonder why. After all, she had betrayed me. Even worse, after her outing with GB she must have known where I was and that I was a prisoner. Yet she still hadn't turned supergrass. Clearly, I'd been wrong ever to think of her as a super-girl. Yet still I wasn't furious with her. Was I still clutching at the straw of her innocence? Maybe my mind reached out for her just to ask her: traitor or un-knowing go-between? Or, when it came to Lisa, perhaps I was just the forgiving kind. In those terrible days of kidnapping and abuse, I'd have accepted her on any terms: real or imaginary, treacherous or true. Even a false Lisa was better than my real life.

I didn't rule out the effect of the drug either. I was strangely detached and subdued (apart from the attack on the door). In character I'd never been particularly volatile but neither had I been that placid before. The drug might be anaesthetizing me to the crimes perpetrated against me, by Lisa and/or her father. After all, brain-washing was the name of the game.

My brain calmly meditated, my spirit (for want of a better organism) went out in search of Lisa, and my body stayed right where it was – wasting in a hut. This time I could feel all three things going on at the same time. My doctor (as I came to call the man who supervised my drug intake) must have gone because my blindfold had been removed. I could see Frank prowling around the hut like a tiger in a cage. Just beyond him there was a window through which I made out that same Pennine valley. I got to my feet slowly, hoping that Frank would think that I had little energy. I stretched and yawned. Then I took off. Just as I'd made a dash for the door, I ran for the window. Frank leapt across the room and dived at me in an attempted rugby tackle. I jumped over his lunging arms, took two more strides then dived through the window. Glass shattered all around me and I landed in a heap, but unhurt, on the grass. Expecting Frank to come after me, I picked myself off the ground and ran away towards the hamlet as quickly as I could. The funny thing was that I ran not because I was afraid of being chased but because of the thrill of it, and the sheer delight of being outside the confines of the hut. My spirit was free, my brain content, but my body took no part. Some part of me still recognized that I hadn't escaped, that there wasn't a window in the hut, that the rugby tackle *had* brought me down.

Well, which of the options would you have followed in those circumstances? Would you have become a joyful armchair drifter or would you have fought the effect of the drug and tried to remain a bored house-bound hostage? Like me, you would have thought, Sod it! I'm not sitting around in the stale atmosphere of a miserable hut. I've been given a vehicle to get away from it for a while. I'm off. Soft option or not.

So please don't blame me for swimming with the tide rather than fighting against it.

I dashed along the path beside the river at the bottom of the hill, across the bridge and up the path into the village. Pub on my left, farmyard and camp-site on my right. No sign of any people at all. I stopped in the middle of the narrow road. It was like the main street of a frontier town just before high noon. Hot, still and expectant. But I could hear noises. Nothing clear – like the sound of the sea in a shell held to the ear. Were the sounds in my ears only or were there real voices? Perhaps people talking about me behind the closed doors of the pub. I didn't know.

Then there was movement. At the other end of the village, a figure walked across the road and disappeared behind a house. Immediately I took off once again, sure that it was Lisa. I stopped and looked round at the point where she had crossed the road. There was no sign of her but there was the footpath to the station. She must have taken it. I ran down the path to a stile. From there, I could see the figure mounting a second stile at the other side of the field. I shouted. No response.

By the time that I'd reached the second stile, the figure had turned behind the signal box and on to the platform. Again I rushed after her, the noise in my ears growing all the time.

I ran faster and faster as I approached the station. The trouble was that, when I got to the signal box, I was going too fast to take the corner on to the platform. Suddenly I realized two things. The noise was due to a train: Manchester to Sheffield, non-stopping. Secondly, I was going to fall on to the line. I put out my arm to grab at a lamppost. I missed it and stumbled. Then someone jumped out from behind the signal box and grabbed me.

"Watch out!" he shouted. "You nearly fell!"

It was Frank's voice and Frank's arms that encircled me.

"You stopped me!" I shouted. "Stopped me from seeing her."

"You might have hurt yourself," Frank said, letting me go.

I felt a fool. A confused fool standing there in the hut, uttering gibberish. But Frank had awoken my sense of outrage. First he'd prevented my meeting Lisa. He'd dragged me back to the hut and reality. Now he was showing sympathy when he was causing all my problems in the first place. It was time for the worm to turn.

"Oh dear! I might have grazed my knee," I said with sarcasm. "Or cut my elbow. What do you care, after what you've done to me?"

"Lie down," Frank said. "That's my advice. Lie down and calm down."

"Don't pretend to be concerned about me now."

"Do you want me to leave for a while?" he asked.

"I never want to see you again!"

After he'd gone, I ranted and raved aloud for a while then I took his advice and lay down. I was exhausted. But I felt too sick to sleep. I felt as if I'd been out in that fierce sunshine for too long. My skin tingled unpleasantly, it almost burned. Any contact with my body gave me a searing pain, so I stripped off all my clothes. At least, I think that's what I did. But then I felt cold. It was probably night-time. I shivered.

> *My emotions bared*
> *It makes me so scared –*
> *How long must this go on?*
> *How long?*
> *How long?*
>
> *Life is suspended*
> *Easily ended*
> *How long can this go on?*
> *How long?*
> *How long?*
>
> *I feel I've grown old*
> *My body so cold*
> *I feel like I could die*
> *No one to care*
> *No one to share*
> *This journey through endless night.*

Yes, I was scared. Scared about what would happen to me. Scared of not knowing, scared of finding out. Terrified of the possibilities. Perhaps I *would* die. They'd pump me so full of dope that my body simply couldn't take any more. I went to my *en suite* toilet and threw up.

Chapter 12

I realize the futility of building up the suspense to a possible fatality. After all, I am here writing the damned story. So you know the outcome right now. I will survive. But I am trying to convey my feelings during that phase of the kidnap and at times I felt that I was going to die.

There's no need for me to chronicle every fantasy, every insanity and every injection. Let me summarize the way things progressed in general terms before giving you some instances that seemed important to me or significant at the time. The whole business seemed like an uphill struggle to an all-time low. I only felt good after a visit from my doctor. I came to welcome his visits. Slowly, I became dependent on him to put me out of my misery. In the end, they didn't have to hold or tie me down to force the stuff into me – I offered myself for it. My whole life revolved around getting my fill of the good doctor's medicine. But in generalizing, I find myself racing ahead again. To purge myself, and to entertain you, I must give you some details. Not every little incident that I endured – not even all the big ones – just the edited highlights, as you might say.

I did get to meet her. Lisa, that is. On a train back to Sheffield. We sat side by side and I loved every moment of it. Okay, so it wasn't real. No flesh-and-blood Lisa, no train to take me home. But if the drug told me that my arm was around her shoulder, that her hand was on my leg, that it was just like it used to be, I wasn't going to argue. We kissed.

"It's good," she said, "to see you again. Haven't seen you for a while."

"No. You can thank your dad for that."

"Dad?"

"Yes. You know."

"No," she said. "I don't see how he's important to you and me."

"You're very loyal to him, then."

Lisa shrugged. "He's my father."

I frowned. "What's that supposed to mean?"

"Don't you just love 'em and hate 'em?" she replied. "Fathers have their good points and their bad."

"Oh?" I said, prompting for more.

She squeezed my leg. "We've talked about him for long enough. You won't wheedle any more out of me."

"Ah," I said, "you are loyal, then."

"No more than the next man."

The train lurched and my hand, dangling in front of her, brushed against her breast. For no good reason, we burst into a childish fit of giggling. The good humour lasted till we got off the train at Dore. There I came down to earth with the proverbial bump. Frank was waiting for us. "Oh, hello, Frank," Lisa said, apparently not displeased to see him. I said nothing at all.

She let go of my hand and went to his side. "Well," she said to me, "it was great to see you again, Seb." I still said nothing. "But we must be off now."

She put her arm around him – yes, she put her arm around Frank – and walked away with him.

I can't tell you what that did to me. I stood there, like a fool, watching them walk away. I didn't move till they disappeared from view. In fact, I can't remember moving even then, but I did because the next thing I recall was lying on the mattress. Lying, head over the edge, feeling wretched and retching.

When I felt that my legs would support me, I stood

up and walked shakily towards the sink. I didn't quite make it, having to grab the kitchen chair to support myself. My head was bursting with noise, my mouth vile and acidic. "Oh, hell!" I shouted. (Toned down version of the true yell.) I lifted the chair above my head and crashed it down on the table, then staggered to the sink. I splashed my face liberally with water. Without drying myself, I slid to the floor, dripping with water and tears.

It was then that I remembered my attempts at graffiti on the inside panel of the unit that I was leaning against. I reached up for a plastic tool from the draining board and continued with my work, scratching at the wood with fury and futility. I was so engrossed in it that I didn't hear Frank come in. I simply became aware of an audience behind me. "Very nice," he said over my shoulder.

"I . . . er . . ." I didn't know what to say. "I'm carving my name. Hope you don't mind."

"Not at all," he said. "But it won't be a message in a bottle, if that's what you had in mind. We'll burn the place down after . . . we've finished with it." He looked around and commented on the kitchen chair lying on its side with a broken rib at the back. "You took it out on the chair rather than on me," he said. "I'm grateful."

Yes, it reminded me that I was furious with him. But he was right, I'd wasted my anger on the chair and cupboard. "I need him, Frank. When's he coming? These noises in my head. I feel awful."

"Sit in the chair and close your eyes. I'll call him."

I escaped the next day. Or at least I think that I did. I can't be sure. (Sounds like the opening of that Camus novel.) Let me just tell you what happened.

In the moments of lucidity and inspiration straight after an injection, my mind swept around the room looking for weapons. The light bulb. I could take it out of the socket, smash it and use the jagged glass on Frank as he came in. But I ruled it out. I wasn't capable of thrusting glass at anyone, not even Frank. Also, when the light was off, he always turned it on before anything else. When it failed to come on, he'd be suspicious straight away. How about the guitar? Could I use it to deliver a blow? No. It was too unwieldy and light to pack much of a punch. Maybe if I'd had a good solid electric guitar . . . but not my acoustic one. My mind turned to the guitar strings. But if I wasn't capable of stabbing anyone, I certainly wouldn't be able to creep up behind him, throw a string over his head, around his neck and slowly throttle him with it.

Then it struck me. There *was* a weapon in the room after all. One that I did feel capable of using. An unlikely weapon, maybe, but a potent one nonetheless. A chemical weapon, you might say. My mind stored away the idea as useful information until I could put it to use. I couldn't turn the theory into practice immediately because of the effects of the injection.

By that time, the pleasures, the meetings with Lisa, the ecstasy weren't lasting as long as the horrors that followed them. This particular session was a nightmare, beginning to end. I won't bother you with it all but basically it was all about moths. You already know that I have a phobia about moths. There's probably a medical term for it. Anyway, I don't mind spiders, snakes seem elegant to me, and I quite like rats. But moths . . . Well, we all have our peculiarities. And for me, having a hut full of moths, seeing a girlfriend covered in moths and breathing moths into my mouth and lungs wasn't a bundle of laughs. I don't feel like recording any more of this appalling experience.

When it was over, I hatched my plot. I waited in the dark behind the door, with a cupful of chemical weapon at the ready. It seemed an age before I heard Frank's footsteps. My heart beat madly as he undid the padlock then unlocked the door. I wasn't sure what the disinfectant from the chemical loo would do exactly, but I reckoned that it would put Frank's eyes out of action for a while.

The door opened and Frank's hand reached round and turned on the light. He stepped into the room and began to close the door. Then I shouted "Frank!" He swung round and looked at me. I threw the liquid into his face, aiming for the eyes. Immediately he yelled out and clutched at his head. It had worked. I hardly hesitated. I ran round the incapacitated Frank and out of the room. There was a short corridor, one door off to a room on the left and another door at the end. This second one looked like an exterior door so I made for it. I couldn't open it though. Either it was stiff or it was locked. A glance over my shoulder reminded me of the fate awaiting me in that room and the sound of water meant Frank was washing away my liquid weapon. I needed no further encouragement. I took a step back then kicked with all my strength at the door. It flew open and there, in front of me, was the real world, bright with evening sun. I took a deep breath and then leapt into some sort of junkyard. To both left and right I saw rows of cars, piled six high. I chose to go to the left. Really, I knew that I had to get to a break in the walls of cars and slip through, out of sight, before Frank emerged from the hut. Yet the row seemed endless. I ran, but soon tired. Obviously I was out of condition. When, eventually, I got to the end of the alley with walls made of cars I stopped and looked back. I hadn't been fast enough because, there, just coming out of the hut, was Frank. He saw me, appeared to shake his head, then began to charge towards me. I shot round the corner to get out of his view and found myself in another row bounded by more stacks of cars. It struck me that I was in a maze with hedges made from smashed cars. How would I ever get out? Or were the walls real at all? Was the chase real? I didn't know, but I had to keep going on the off-chance that it *was* real.

This new alley was just like the other one. Everywhere, cars piled high and the path littered with bits of metal, glass, plastic – all, I guessed, from dilapidated cars. From somewhere behind me came the sound of Frank's footsteps crunching on the debris as he pounded after me. This time I did spot a gap between two stacks of battered cars and I darted through it into a parallel alley. I didn't run anywhere, though, I simply propped myself against a rusting wreck (quite appropriate considering that I was a decaying wreck myself). I knew that in my state I wouldn't be able to outrun him so I had to play tricks if I was to escape. I stood there trying to stop my panting sounding so loud, hoping and praying that he wouldn't see me.

His footsteps got louder, then stopped for a while. He'd reached the corner, no doubt, and was deciding what to do. Then he set off again, running. I held my breath as he came level with the cars that I was hiding behind. But there was no need, my ploy had worked. He ran straight past. I sighed. By this time, I was convinced that it was real, that at long last I was outside that dingy hut. The chase seemed real enough. The car that I was propped against seemed solid, but there again, so did Lisa when I had my arm round her. I tried to stop my mind drifting. I needed to concentrate on stealth, not on Lisa.

Quietly as I could, I crept down the alley, constantly looking for gaps where I might sneak through to less conspicuous parts of the scrapyard. All the time, listening and watching for Frank. To get through the third gap that I found, I had to shuffle sideways but it paid unexpected dividends. On the other side I found myself at the edge of the maze. There was a wire fence, a field beyond and, in the distance, a road. A real road with real cars driven by real people. People who could help me. I was about one hundred metres from a long track that led from the yard to the road, but I didn't dare just make a bid for it because there was no cover at all. I slipped back through the gap. I could get closer to the exit more surreptitiously by making my way towards it but behind the last row of empty car shells. I just had to hope that there was another gap nearer to the track that I'd seen.

Again, as furtively as possible, I crept down the small path between two rows of cars. When I reached the point opposite the track there was no gap to slip through, but just a little further down the alley there was a place where the cars gave way to a pile of junk, about waist high. I had only to scramble over it, across a bit of open yard and down the track to the main road. But, unless I was very careful, it was going to be noisy over the pile of car parts. It was my best chance, though.

I made my way to the end of the wall of cars then paused for a while. The only noise was the distant and reassuring rumble of cars. I stepped out from behind the wall and there, on the other side, stood Frank. Beyond him was the track and freedom.

Looking straight at me, he said, "Give up, Seb. You haven't got an earthly." He stepped towards me onto the pile of rubbish.

I was so close to escape but . . . No. I decided to go down fighting for once. I bent down and picked up the first thing that came to hand. It was big and heavy. A cylinder head, I should think. I don't know what possessed me – desperation I guess – but I threw it at him. Like me, Frank seemed amazed. For an instant his face betrayed disbelief. By the time that he'd accepted that I'd done it, it was too late. He jumped aside, avoiding the worst of it, but he still took a blow on the hip. He shouted, lost his footing and collapsed in a heap, useless like the rest of the junk.

I clambered over the pile and across the yard. Frank showed no sign of getting to his feet but even so I ran as fast as I could down the rough track. By the time I got to the main road I was breathless and distraught. I dashed headlong into the road, not mindful of the danger, and flagged down the first car that I saw. Luckily it was only going slowly. The driver, a man, leaned across the front seat and said through the open window, "What's wrong, sonny?"

I know that I hate being called "sonny" but the simple question and concerned tone sounded like heaven to me. I don't know what I replied but it was probably garbled. Something about being chased, kidnapped, drugged. "Okay," he said. "Get in the back."

I almost fell into the back of the car. It seemed like luxury. Soon I'd be home. But the relief didn't last long. Instead of screeching away from the place to the nearest hospital or police station, the driver spun the wheel and the car lurched on to the track up to the junkyard. "Where are you going?" I shrieked. He didn't answer. I yanked desperately on the handle but could not open the door. "Don't bother," the man said. "Child-proof locks." This time I recognized the voice. It was my doctor, no doubt on his way to my next appointment.

I collapsed on to the seat. "Oh no!" I'd blown it. What's more, it dawned on me that I was *really* going to cop it. Frank and the doctor were hardly the forgiving kind – I knew that they'd make me suffer for my little escapade. I dreaded the next injection.

Chapter 13

I was lying on the mattress in the dark, my mind was clear and fertile. Next to me, Lisa's warm body slowly rose and fell rhythmically with her breathing. "Are you asleep?" I whispered.

"No," she said.

"I want to ask you something."

"Oh, yes?" She turned to me.

"Why don't they just kill me and have done with it?"

"They don't want to be child murderers," she answered. "Besides, it's also a matter of fitting the punishment to the crime."

"Yes," I said. "I see."

"Come on!" she said, standing up and stepping over me. "No more morbid thoughts. Let me help you up." She offered me both her hands.

I grasped her hands with both of mine and she yanked me to my feet. Naturally, my arms encircled her for support. I clung to her as I clung on to my own sanity. I spoke quietly into her ear, "Their tactics aren't working, Lisa. But don't tell them. It's our secret. You see, they're trying to make me forget who's behind all this. But the more dope they pump into me, the more I think of you – the more I cling to you. It's funny, isn't it? The more drugs they give me, the more refuge I take in you. And you're the key to the whole business. More dope, more Lisa, more connection between me, kidnapping, drugs and the Woodwards. It *is* funny, isn't it?"

She put her hands on my shoulders and pushed a little so my head came off her shoulder and she could look at me. "Sure it's funny," she said, forcing a smile. "But what we've got to do is get you out of here. It's no good retaining your sanity if your body . . ." She paused. "Well, it's filthy in here. Unhealthy."

"Yes. They took away the toilet stuff, you know. I just do it in the bin now. It gets awful smelly. I'm sorry."

"It's not your fault," she said.

"There's a song, you know, not one of Dad's. I can't remember it all but it goes, 'Whatever they do to you, They can't take away your dignity.' Or something like that. But don't you believe it. Its sentiments are about as accurate as its scan. Look at me."

"Yes. Well, that's why you have to get out of here." She shook me by the shoulders. "Concentrate! I've thought of a plan. It's your guitar. You can take one of its strings, or several joined together, and . . ."

"Already thought of it," I interrupted.

"Hear me out," she said. "Fix one end to the door, near the bottom, and the other end to the door post. When Frank comes in through the door, he'll trip over it. And you dash out."

"Sounds dodgy to me. Will it work?"

"Of course it'll work," she encouraged.

I stepped back from her. "How can I trust you? You went with him." The droning in my ears had returned and I shook my head violently to try to get rid of it, but failed. I pressurized my ears (or whatever yawning does) and the humming ceased for a while.

"But I had to," she said, defending her actions. "Dad made me."

"So how do I know that you're not under orders now?"

"Don't make it worse for me, Seb. I feel guilty for what I've done, without this."

Both of us turned to the door. It was the sound of the key in the lock. "It's Frank," she whispered urgently. "I must go. Remember my plan."

When I turned to protest her departure, she'd already gone. The hut was empty.

"Glad to see you on your feet for a change," Frank said as he closed the door.

"Frank, I . . ."

"Yes?"

"I won't do it again. I need a proper toilet in here. It gets . . ." I was lost for a word that was bad enough.

"Unpleasant?" Frank suggested. "Well, you brought it on yourself. Come on," he said, "slopping out time. In a 'proper toilet', as you call it, out here. That's the best I can offer you."

The second escape, I'm sure was imagined. Lisa's plan was too far-fetched and fanciful to be real. And after it was all over, my guitar had not been taken away from me, and it was replete with all its strings. Anyway I carried out the plan, though I don't know how I fixed the string to the wooden door. That's another reason for believing it to be fantasy. The final reason revolved around what happened – or more correctly, appeared to happen – after Frank had fallen and I'd run out.

I found myself on the golf course near my house, and I don't mean my hut, I mean our house. Flude Acres. Below me, there was the spot on Abbey Lane where the kidnap began. The area was cordoned off and three men, presumably policemen, were on their knees combing the ground. At first I smiled. I was right. The cavalry was out looking for clues. But after a moment's thought I felt disdain. They'd got no idea! What did they hope to find in the road? Or perhaps they were merely praying. They weren't getting anywhere, in any event. So much for my early optimism about legions of the police force's best officers on the job. I looked up to the heavens as if asking for patience. "They should be surrounding the hut with crack shots," I said to the sky, "not scratching around in the road looking for tyre prints." When I looked back to the road, they'd gone. There was not even a trace of evidence that they had been there at all. Perhaps it was a forlorn hope that even fruitless energy was being expended on my behalf. No, I dismissed the thought. "They're out there somewhere. They just need a lead, that's all."

I ran down the hill, across Abbey Lane, and up the path by the railway bridge. You know where I was headed, don't you? Home, via my beautiful familiar wood. I wondered what would happen, what Mum and Dad would say and do, when I sauntered in through the back door saying, "Good day. Long time no see. How've you been keeping?" No, you're right, I wouldn't have kept my cool, of course. I'd have disgraced myself and gone in running, shouting, crying. "Mum! Dad!" I'd have thrown myself at Mum and blurted out the whole story. Lots of gushing, no doubt. No sign of the stiff upper lip any more. But there would have been a special type of closeness and . . . well . . . love that's only felt after being deprived of it for what seemed like an eternity. After all, they weren't bad parents, you know. (I was going to cross out these last few sentences as sentimental drivel but Miss Greene told me not to. "Don't be afraid of your feelings, Seb," she said. "There's nothing to be ashamed of.")

I took the same narrow path that I did in chapter one. In my head, the hum of some machine or giant lorry sounded. Every time I stopped walking and turned my head to try to locate the source of the noise, it went away. I was within sight of THE oak tree when the droning came back with a vengeance and refused to go away. Then I realized, as I had once before, that it was simply a train. Coming into Sheffield from Manchester. The same one that Lisa and I had been on. Yet after the train had rushed through the wood, the noise persisted in my head. I tried to carry on. After all, I must have been within two hundred metres of our house. Twenty seconds for a decent athlete. But it seemed an age to me. By the time that I reached that fateful tree, I had to stop. The noise had reached a crescendo with screams, pounding drums, police sirens, cries of pain. My head was fit to burst. And all the yawning and shaking in the world wouldn't shift it. I leaned against the oak. I couldn't make my triumphant return home in this state, I had to take drastic measures to stop that awful racket. I turned and, on some weird impulse, banged my head against the trunk of the tree. Well, I thought it was a good idea at the time. It didn't help a great deal but perhaps a little, so I butted the tree again. And again. I stood there like a demented head-banger at an Iron Maiden gig, thumping myself against the tree in time to a pounding that only I could hear. And I carried on till I could feel the blood running down my cheeks and nose.

The next thing I felt was someone pulling me away from the tree to stop me hurting myself further. I blinked, trying to clear my vision. What I saw horrified me. There was the edge of the sink, running red with blood. All the way down the cupboard door and dripping onto the floor. "Oh, no!" someone uttered. It was probably me. Then I passed out.

It was sheer luxury to be back in my floating state. No cares in the world. No pain. No noise at all. Just calmness.

It didn't last, though. Someone was shaking me, telling me that I must remain conscious. Heaven knows why. I didn't want to see reality again. It wasn't much fun.

"Get off!" I said.

"No. Talk to me. Swear at me, if you like."

"Leave me alone."

"No. You need attention. Until the doctor arrives, I'll clean you up. But you need stitches." I was manhandled into a chair. Then the voice said, "What the bloody hell got into you?"

Suddenly, I realized what had happened. I *had* got home. It was Dad, nit-picking in my hair again. "I was hoping to slip upstairs and do it myself," I told him. "I didn't want you to see."

"So you're ashamed, but what happened?"

"It was a bus. Number 26. I heard its engine in my head. I ran out in front of it."

"Okay, Seb. Just keep still. I'll clean it up. Quite some gashes here, though. We'll need more than water."

"Big bus, the 26," I mumbled. While Dad dabbed delicately at my head, I drifted pleasantly in and out of consciousness, comforted by the wonderful feeling of being safely at home again. I only needed some stitches and a little time to recuperate and everything would be normal once more.

I became aware of someone entering the room. Mum, I assumed. "What's going on?" But it was a man's voice, not Mum's. "I told you not to call me at the surgery."

"Look," the first voice said, sounding less like Dad than before. "It's urgent."

"Oh, great! I thought it was your job to stop this sort of damage. I don't suppose there's any chance of taking him to hospital, is there?" There was a pause. "Here, then," my doctor said. "Take this. You'll have to help patch him up."

"Okay," Frank said.

Frank! It had never been Dad. I'd just been delirious. I'd never been at home. I can't tell you how I felt at that moment. Disappointed is hardly the word for it. Devastated perhaps. I'll say devastated and hurt, and leave it at that. I'll tell you about the physical effects, if you like. My head ached. Not the sort of ache that aspirin fixes. The sort of ache that's one step short of unbearable. An ache that doesn't go away or show any sign of easing. And on top of the ache, there were stabs of pain. The sort of pain that brings tears to your eyes even when you don't cry. Maybe it was caused by whatever my doctor was doing. I put my hand up to feel my head, but it got slapped by someone. "Don't touch, you silly bugger." Lovely bedside manner, my doctor had.

Suddenly there was a fierce, penetrating, excruciating pain as if someone had seared my wounds with a hot iron. For the instant in which I remained conscious, I thought that my time had come. I could write pages on my feelings in that split-second, but I'll only indulge myself a little. I felt hopeless and helpless. I had nothing – no family, no Lisa, no home. I didn't know where I was. I was not altogether sure who I was. I'd had so much dope that my senses were worthless. What use was someone who couldn't tell fact from fiction, a tree from a sink, and a good idea from a bad one? No one was rushing to rescue me. Perhaps I'd been forgotten as well as abused and betrayed. And on top of that, I thought that I was dying. Was it worth fighting any more? Everything went black.

Chapter 14

"Come on. Wake up."

"What?"

"Wake up."

"I feel awful."

"Yes, I know. But if you will try to do a Psycho in the sink, what can you expect?"

"I can't move my head."

"You'll live."

"It doesn't feel like it. I need," I paused, "I need help."

"You'll get help soon. But first you must eat."

"I'm not hungry."

"You must eat sometime, Seb." Frank sounded concerned. "It's been a long time."

I felt weak and empty but food wasn't at the top

of my list of priorities. My bandaged head throbbed and my whole body ached. For some reason, I imagined that somehow I'd been drained of blood and now a venom ran in my veins, its poison infiltrating every little part of me. I needed an injection of new blood. "No food," I muttered. "Just help."

I was yanked into a sitting position and something mushy was forced into my mouth. I coughed and spluttered but some of it found its way down past my throat, I suppose. Once the struggle was over and I'd been fed like an unwilling baby, I got my reward. Eagerly, I raised my arm for the doctor to give me the elixir of life.

It was night, but in front of me the blackness was dispelled by flames. I sat crosslegged on one side of the flames. On the other side, separated from me by fire, sat Lisa. Sometimes I could see her, sometimes not, as the breeze swayed the flames first one way then the other. "You know what we should do around the campfire," she said through the flames. "It's traditional to have a sing-song." I said nothing. I was still suffering, still sore about everything, still unsure about the value of struggling on. "Come on," she urged, "there's nothing like a good airing of your 'Ging Gang Goolies'." She smiled tentatively at me. "Okay," she conceded, "we'll do an Afterglow instead. You play, I'll try to sing. 'I'll give you strength'." I played – rather mechanically – while she sang pointedly.

> *Power and money vitalize*
> *Indifferent to despairing eyes.*
> *Need*
> *Subordinated to greed.*
>
> *You've been used, broken, cast aside*
> *Tortured till your parents cried.*
> *Fight*
> *Don't take your life this night.*
>
> *Want you to wake in the morning*
> *Hear your wasted body breathing.*
> *Dear,*
> *Believe me I will be here.*
>
> *I'll give you strength, I will stay,*
> *Even underdogs have their day.*
> *Fight*
> *Don't take your life this night.*

Okay, it wasn't the most suble act on her behalf but maybe it made me feel a little better. She cared. She at least was trying. When the last note had drifted away there was nothing but the crackling of the fire.

I looked through the flames at her. Even with

shadows and light playing tricks with her face, she looked wonderful. "Lisa," I asked, "did you really set me up that night?"

She was looking into the fire, then she glanced up at me. Quickly her eyes darted back to the flames. "Yes," she said quietly.

"Why?"

She picked up a stick and poked the fire with it. All at once, the crackling of the campfire became in my ears more like the ferocious roar of a furnace. I saw her lips moving but I heard nothing but the thundering in my head. "Oh, no!" I shouted. "Not again."

I felt two people at my sides, each taking an arm and pulling me up, dragging me away, then dropping me into a chair. My head hit the back of the chair and I screamed. I opened my eyes and saw two faces staring into mine. I think it was Frank and my doctor. The noise had gone and I heard one of them addressing me. "No more histrionics. Sit there a while. Rest. You'll be okay." I closed my eyes and dozed.

I awoke to a crashing noise. The door of the hut burst open as if it had been kicked. A man stood in the doorway. "Sebastian," he called into the darkness of the hut. "Sebastian Flude?"

"Yes," I replied cautiously. I was getting suspicious in my premature old age.

"You're here?"

"Yes."

The man came and stood somewhere in front of me. "What have they been doing to you?"

"Nothing. I did it myself."

"Oh. Well, we'll have to get it looked at." His accent was strange but his tone was friendly, kind and businesslike.

"It's dark. I can't see you properly. Who are you?" I asked.

"Sergeant Ross. Call me Eddie."

"Police?" It seemed incredible that a rescue could be as simple as a man kicking in the door and calling out my name.

"That's right," he replied. "Look, we have to be careful. Where are the people who've kept you here? Somewhere near?"

"I don't know."

"Are you expecting them back?"

"I don't know. It's all very irregular. Confusing."

"Well, who are they? Do you know names?"

"Frank. That's all. But it's not his real name."

"Why's he keeping you here? Did he say?"

"He said lots."

"Can you remember?"

"My head hurts," I think I said. I told myself that my head was irrelevant, that I must keep to the point. The police were here and I had to do my bit to help if we were going to finish the business there and then. "Er. Yes. Punishment.

Punishing Dad for not being a courier."

"Courier of what?"

"Drugs," I said. "Crack, I think."

"Who was your dad working for?"

"How do you mean?" I hesitated. "He was working for you."

"No," the policeman said, "who was behind the drugs ring?"

"How should I know?"

"You might have heard something. Maybe this . . . Frank let something slip."

"No. But I *did* hear something."

"What? What did you hear?" he asked excitedly.

"I heard a dog."

"What?"

"A dog."

"Yes? And?" he prompted.

"Well," I struggled to say it. I didn't really want to get her into trouble but when the crunch came I knew that I'd have to take sides. The beans would have to be spilled. "It was Lisa's dog."

"I see," the man said. "You've been very helpful. Look. Stay there. I'll have to get a doctor before I can move you. Okay? Stay there."

The light went on at last and I could look around. But search as I might, there was no one in the room but Frank. No policeman, no cavalry. No SAS-style rescue. I groaned. "Yes," he said, as if confirming that groaning was the correct response. "I hoped it would be all over by now as well. I thought it had gone far enough. But apparently not."

Did I laugh and joke, "You can get done for impersonating a police officer"? No. I said, "Why, Frank? Why punish me like this?"

Frank shook his head. "We never meant to hurt you. Only your father. You brought it on yourself."

I nodded. "What is it you're giving me, anyway?"

"Oh," Frank said somewhat hesitantly. "No one drug. A cocktail, blended especially for you." Clearly, he found the topic uncomfortable. I hoped that it was feelings of guilt rather than a need for secrecy that made him unwilling to say more.

I looked at the floor. Around the legs of my chair there were a few brown stains. Over by the cupboard there were more bloodstains where I'd performed my headbanging ritual. The mattress also showed some giveaway brown marks. "How's my head?" I asked.

"You'll live."

"It's the noises, you see. I . . ."

He interrupted. "You don't have to explain to me. Anyway," he added, "it's time for food now."

I did manage to swallow something. To this day, I don't know what it was though. Everything that was pushed into my mouth tasted like stewed apple, but it could have been anything. It didn't matter anyway because, if experience was anything to go by, most of it would reappear a little later. (A delicate turn of phrase, I think you'll agree.)

"I'm hot," I complained. "Hot and sweaty."

"I'll put the fan on for you." The blades clattered a little then settled to a contented purr.

"I don't suppose it's any use to ask if you know how Mum and Dad are."

"That's nothing to do with me," Frank said. "I'm only interested in you."

When my GP arrived, there was no need for blindfolding or keeping eyes tightly closed. He didn't exactly advertise his presence, preferring to be out of my sight as much as possible, but I'd seen his face. The damage had been done as far as my bent doctor was concerned. He seemed disgruntled, but he still kept the appointments. They must have been paying him well.

This particular visit was special. As soon as the needle punctured my arm, I knew that there was something special about it. There was an almost immediate sense of well-being, such as I'd never felt before. After the recent horrors, it was ecstasy. And I mean ecstasy. I can't describe it but it was such a wonderful feeling of harmony that nothing else mattered to me. It was like experiencing all my favourite, spine-tingling things at the same time and then on top of that, feeling the sense of achievement and satisfaction that would accompany fulfilling all my ambitions and fantasies. Not bad, eh? It seemed to last only a couple of minutes but after it had gone, I felt that I would do *anything* to let my body feel that way again, to experience perfection again.

On my way down from the peak, I heard raised voices in the room. "Yes, but I decided to step it up to get it over with."

"I don't suppose," Frank rejoined, "that it's got anything to do with the fact that he can identify you."

"I'm just trying to complete my contract."

"What'll happen to him?"

"A few minutes of exhilaration, they say. Followed by depression, preoccupation with death. That sort of thing."

"Go on. Get out," Frank snapped. "You've done enough damage. I'll stay till he's stable."

What I heard didn't surprise or shatter me. First I copped it because, through GBH, I could identify Woodward as Mr Big. Then I copped it again because I could identify a rogue doctor. And, if you think back over the last few episodes, you would note that death was already becoming a favourite theme of my drug-induced dreams. So I didn't need to be told about my fetish as if it were something new. My blood was being drained from my body and replaced with venom, but I'd seen it all before. No, I didn't hear anything that perturbed me.

I sat there in that dark, dingy, smelly hut and

stared around me, stared with cocaine eyes, without really seeing anything but the blankness, the walls that hemmed me in and the whirring fan. I hated that hut. And yet I loved it as well. Because if I ever left it, who would give me my medicine? Who would get me high? I wanted to break out and I wanted to stay.

Deserted
In a strangely barren land.
Solitude embraces me
But the wind is howling round.
Chill wind. Chill wind.

Nothing heard
Spirits soaring undisturbed.
A breathless isolation
Till the shrill wind rushes by.
Shrill wind. Shrill wind.

All alone
All my feelings turn to stone.
When the wind begins its roar
Blasts my flesh down to the bone.
Ill wind. Ill wind.

Set me free.
I can't take a minute more.
Let me find my way back home
But who's there to help me soar?
Chill wind. Ill wind.

I stood up and the stream of air from the fan was directed straight into my face. At first it merely cooled, but as I took a step forward it began to chill. Another step and the noise of the fan grew louder. The draught became a gust and it felt as if it was blasting away layers of skin from my face. I put my hand out towards the blades to try to deflect the flow but it froze my hand. As the strength of the wind increased further, the humming of the blades began to sound like the scream of an aeroplane's propeller. I had trouble keeping on my feet, swaying in the current of air. I leaned towards it and took a step forward. My hand had turned blue but I kept it outstretched because I believed that if I pushed it into the spinning blades, then I could stop the deafening noise and the numbing wind. Another metre, another step, and my fingers could grasp them. The wind seemed directed against my whole body then and not just my face. My shirt billowed. My trousers pressed against my legs at the front and flapped about at the back. I lifted my foot to move forward again but the blast was too strong for me. It lifted me off my feet and flung me backwards. I shot across the hut and slammed into the door. The roar of the fan ceased but my head . . . It was fit to burst. I felt the blood on my face again and blackness descended.

Blows to my head are the recurring theme in this

story, you'll have noticed. But this one really got to me. I must have thought that, in opening up the wound again, I'd ruined my chances of ever being healed. I sat, a dirty crumpled bleeding mess on the floor, and cried.

"Hey, come on," someone said, putting his arm around me. "It's not worth it."

I looked up at the man. "Dad!" I exclaimed.

"Come on. I'll help you get up if you like."

I was so pleased to see him again that I cried again. "I . . ." I didn't really know what else to say.

"It's all right," he said. "You don't have to say anything if you don't want to."

"It's punishment, Dad," I blurted out. "Do you know what they've done to me?"

"Yes. I know. I feel . . . Well, I'm sorry, Seb."

"It's okay. You did right." Then a thought struck me. "How's Mum? Where is she?"

"I . . . um . . ." It was Dad's turn to lose the right words. He turned his eyes away from me, then looked back into my face. "She's been punished too, Seb."

"What?"

"She's been . . ."

I pushed him away and he toppled over on to the floor. "It's all your fault," I screamed at him.

"No, Seb. Don't . . ." His voice trailed away as he tumbled across the room and faded into the blackness.

I was really reaching my lowest ebb. If there had been a decent bit of Sheffield steel in the room, I'd have finished it right then. I really would. What was the point of not doing so? Then I heard Lisa. "No," she said. "Don't. 'I'll give you strength.' Remember?"

"What's this?" I asked sceptically as she stepped out of the shadows. "More betrayal, or solace?"

"Don't be like that, Seb. I . . ."

I didn't give her an opportunity to continue. "Why shouldn't I be like that? I've been through enough. And you're as guilty as the rest. Well, aren't you?"

"Yes," she said, her head bowed. "You want me to go?"

"Yes . . . No. I don't want to see you like this. I don't want you to see me like this. I don't trust you. I can't trust you."

As soon as she'd stepped back into the shadows, I realized what I'd done. I'd sent away two people who really cared. "Lisa!" I shouted. "Lisa?" But there was no reply. I rose shakily to my feet and staggered in the direction that I thought she'd taken. I tripped over something – a chair maybe – but didn't quite fall. My hands grasped something solid and hung on. "Lisa!" I called again. No, she'd gone. I'd sent away the only one who had kept me sane. Who'd prevented Frank and the doctor emptying my memory. Well, that was it, the famous last straw. Beam me up, Scotty, I've had enough. I gripped tight on the edge of the sink and prepared to bring my head down on it as hard as I could.

> Gave it my best try
> But the first hurdle
> Proved too much for me.
> Kiss my love goodbye.
> As I become memory
> I wonder if she'll miss me
> Her faller
> Faller at the first hurdle.

Somewhere in the room there was a shriek. "No!" My body was yanked and dragged, then bundled into a chair. I was very confused but I realized that I was being strapped into the armchair. "Yes," I said. "Yes. Help. I need help."

"No. I'm doing it for your own good. If . . ." he hesitated, "anyone wants to complete this job, he can bloody well do it himself! Stay there. Out of harm's way, while I go and . . . make a report." Frank stepped away from the chair and disappeared from view. That was the third person to run out on me in a matter of minutes!

I don't know how long I remained in the armchair. Half the time I was convinced that I was elsewhere anyway. A bit of rope can't restrain imagination. No, not even I could control my imagination. If I'd had any control at all, I wouldn't have seen or felt any of the things that I experienced as I sat there. Aloud I said, "Think of . . . ten-pin bowling with Lisa, the open air, the Peak District, my lime tree. Anything except . . ." but I continued to see and feel the moths on me, inside my clothing, on my face. I also saw Mum and Dad as they sat, silent and grief-stricken, in our lounge. I saw anonymous hoodlums creeping through the wood, closing in on our house. I watched as other crooks dug a grave by that famous oak tree, and incompetent policemen lurked behind other trees but did nothing. I saw Frank and Lisa together in her bedroom. Need I go on? I think you've got the idea. Oh, just one more thing. I saw another police rescue acted out in front of me. But I was wise to it this time. Frank had made his report and Woodward had sent another bogus policeman to test me. To see how I'd reacted to the last big dose.

The door caved in and there in front of me was an outline of a man. He shouted over his shoulder, "Jim! In here. Bring your kit."

He knelt by me and undid the rope. "You're okay now. Do you hear?" I said nothing. I just stared at him suspiciously. He glanced up at a second man – Jim – who was fiddling about in my hair. "Well?"

Jim's voice, oozing with feigned concern, came over my head. "He needs hospital treatment, Ross."

Not Sergeant Ross again! Not very imaginative. "Not quite yet," he said. And that's when I knew the catch was coming. "How many were holding you?" he asked me.

I shrugged. "One."

For some reason, this Ross grabbed my arms and held them up, I think for Jim to see them. I pulled them back. "Get off," I growled. I tried to concentrate so as not to be tricked again. But I knew that I was drifting. I only caught fragments of the conversation and only answered a few of their questions. But I reckoned that feeling brain-dead was to my advantage.

"He's hardly with us."

"What was his name?"

"Get these moths off me and I'll tell you."

"Ross, we really must take him."

"Okay. Just a second. Seb, who was behind it? Help us to help you, Seb. Please. Who was it?"

"He isn't in a fit state to help, Ross. Just get him out of here."

"All right. Get them organized outside."

Sentences, the whirring fan, questions, shouts. I heard them all, going round in my head, amplifying with each cycle. It was happening again! That hideous noise. I stood up, and suddenly made for the door. I had to get out. But Ross was too quick for me. He had me firmly by the shoulders. I sighed submissively. "You're too fast for me," I said. I was bluffing, though. In the next moment, I brought my knee up and caught him where it hurts. His grip loosened and I dashed down that corridor again, towards the open air.

Chapter 15

I opened the door. What I saw stopped me in my tracks. It was night. There were lots of men . . . well, a few. And police cars everywhere . . . well, at least a couple. Blue lights flashing. But were they real? A man stepped in front of me to stop me running off. I felt like a cornered animal, frightened and wounded. Flight, fight or surrender? I was confused and unsure. I turned round to look at Ross and I guess that he saw panic and bewilderment on my face. He stopped a distance from me. Presumably he decided that I would interpret any approach as a threat. He did not wish to alarm me further. "It's all right, Jim," he called to the man behind me. "No problem."

The lights outside cast a pale flickering glow over

my shoulder and on to Sergeant Ross's face. In that light, somehow I recognized him. I'd seen him from my bedroom window. It was the man whose face had been caught by the flame of a match as he lit a cigarette under my lime tree. The man who'd spoken to Dad that night, ages ago. "I . . . you're . . ." I paused, overwhelmed. "You smoke, don't you?" I asked.

"What?"

"You're not Sergeant Ross at all, are you?"

"No. I'm Ross Taylor."

"You're a real policeman!" I could hardly believe it.

He nodded. "As real as they come." Then he did approach me. "Are you okay now? Ready to leave?"

"Leave?" It seemed almost impossible that I could ever exist away from that hut.

Ross smiled. "Yeah. You can leave right now. All right?"

"I don't know. Yes, I think so."

He put his arm around me to help me walk. As we passed Jim, Ross said to him, "You know what to do. Stake it out. Quickly as you can, kill these lights. I'll take him to the hospital. And Jim," he called over his shoulder, "get the bastards that did this. Okay?"

The scrapyard was exactly as I remembered it but in the dark it looked even more eerie than it had before. Ross's car was unmarked, something large like a Volvo. It could even have been the same as my doctor's. Ross opened the door for me, helped me in, and strapped the seat belt around me. After he'd got into the driver's seat, he didn't start the engine straight away. Instead he turned to me and asked, "Want to talk about it?"

"Not really," I said. "But I'll try. You see, I've been in a car before. One like this."

"Oh?"

"He was a doctor. The one who drugged me. It wasn't Frank." I looked at Ross and saw a puzzled look on his face. "I'm not very clear. Sorry."

He put his hand on my knee. "You're doing fine."

"Will Mum and Dad be . . . wherever we're going?"

"I'll send for them, so they can be at the hospital when you've been patched up."

"Are they okay?"

"Sure. I was with them before coming here. They'll be . . . pleased, to put it mildly, to see you. Anyway," he said, starting the car, "we'd better get going. We can talk as we go along. Do you know the name of this bent doctor?"

I shook my head, but it reminded me that it was still very painful when moved. "No. I'd recognize him, though."

"Good. Who's Frank?"

"That's not his real name. He's the one who kidnapped me. Under orders."

"He was acting under orders? Whose orders, Seb? Do you know?" His eyes flashed towards me then back to the road.

"Yes," I said. "I know." Well, the moment had come. The moment to burn all bridges. Only one way forward. The way that led to the destruction of Lisa's family. "Your man's name is Woodward."

Ross nearly drove the car into a brick wall. He stopped and turned to me. "Are you sure? How do you know?"

I held up my arm to him. "Look. I can't stop shaking. And I'm freezing. Will they be able to . . . help me at the hospital?"

"Yes."

"I won't be like this for ever?"

"No. They'll wean you off it. It won't be fun, Seb, but compared to what you've been through . . ." He looked at the top of my head. "That needs fixing up too."

"Guess so."

"How about Woodward?" Ross prompted.

"It's not easy for me to say."

"Okay." He put the car back into gear and pulled away from the kerb. "But before I push the panic button, I must be sure. We know him, of course. Woodward. Totley Brook." Ross paused. "We know his daughter as well." He glanced at me. "Don't we?"

"Lisa." I sighed and closed my eyes. "Lisa. She set me up for the kidnap, didn't she?"

"It crossed our minds. So we interviewed her. After you disappeared. Not me – an experienced policewoman. She was convinced that Lisa *wasn't* involved. And I agree. So . . . if you're right, she's a bloody good actress. She seemed genuinely shocked by your kidnap. And it hit her hard enough to make her quite ill."

"But . . . I can't think straight. She made sure that I left early. Delivered right into their hands."

"She had to be home early. Her dad imposed a deadline – ten-thirty or something. She rowed with him about it."

"Really?" Was that the answer? Was she innocent, just manipulated by her dad? But she hadn't let on when she discovered that I was being held in the hut.

"We wondered about her father, too. Checked him out. Some large bank deposits but, there again, his business is going well. We've nothing solid on him. Clean as far as we're concerned. So," he asked, understandably keen to hear my condemnation, "why do you think it's him?"

I shut my eyes tight as I tried to concentrate on my account. I guess that I still rambled, but the kernel of the story must have emerged.

When I opened my eyes, Ross was speaking into

a microphone of some sort and getting crackly noises back. "Yes. So," he was saying, "there's a company that owns another company that's a front for the company that owns the breaker's yard. It's well disguised. But what's the bottom line? Can you say that one of Woodward's companies is at the end of the chain?" I didn't catch the distorted words of response. "Okay," Ross said. "Send the lot. Not tomorrow. Now!" He put the microphone down and smiled at me. "As soon as I learned where you were I put someone on to tracing the owner of the breaker's yard. It took a while because Woodward's distanced himself from it, but it's him all right. It confirms your story. I've sent the troops to pick him up. You've done us a favour," he said.

"Yeah. Well, you've done me one, too, I guess." Then it struck me that *I* hadn't asked *him* the obvious question. "How did you find me?"

"Intelligence."

"What?"

"A tip-off. Tonight. It came to your mum and dad's house. Where I was. That's how I came to lead the troops."

A tip-off? Who? I asked myself. The question echoed in my mind as if I should be able to figure it out and deduce something important. I found it hard to be logical, though, especially with the noise of the engine drumming in my ears. Ross was saying something. "Not too far to the hospital now." Somewhere a horn sounded – as loud as a fire alarm in my ears. When it stopped resounding in my head, I heard a voice. Not Ross's. Just a solitary voice.

Tempting to think now it will all be plain sailing
Old enough now to know there's no such thing.

"Stop the car!" I shouted.

Ross slammed on the brakes and my head felt as if it was going to roll off my shoulders.

"Why were you with Mum and Dad?" I asked.

"Twenty-four-hour protection."

"Why didn't they come with you? Why aren't they here?" I asked frantically.

"It's all right, Seb. You're safe. You're with me."

"But why didn't they come with you?"

"It's normal. We don't want parents around in operations like this. They can do the silliest things, understandably, in eagerness. It's just standard practice, Seb. I'll call them from the hospital."

"What did you say?"

"I'll call them from the hospital."

"No. Before that," I said.

"What do you mean?"

"Standard practice." I turned to him. "You said 'standard practice'! You mean police routine?"

"If you like, yes."

My head thumped, my spine tingled.

"What's wrong?" Ross asked.

Routine? Routine means predictable. That's what Frank said. And predictability is a weakness to be exploited. My brain battled against the din, the ache and the venom. How could they exploit. . . ? Then it clicked. "Who's left with Mum and Dad?" I asked him.

"How do you mean?"

"You did leave someone with them, didn't you?"

"Yes," Ross said. "We're thin on the ground these days but one of my chaps is there."

"Just one," I moaned. The noises had gone. I felt utterly helpless and empty. Numb. I knew what was happening and the thought choked me. I struggled to find the words to explain it to Ross. "Don't you see?" I said. "You've played into their hands. They were never after *me*."

"What?"

"I'm not the primary victim. It wasn't part of the plan to mess me up. I brought that on myself. They're after Dad, not me. Frank said as much. I'm a decoy, Ross. That's all."

My head hit the back of the seat as the car screeched away. "Hold on!" Ross shouted. "We're not far from your place. I'll divert. All the others will be at the breaker's yard or at the Woodwards'. I'll get help as soon as I can." He picked up the microphone again. "It's Ross. Urgent. Get Mike at the Fludes, will you? Yes. My channel's open." He waited. A minute later the speaker crackled into life. He listened then replied. "No answer. Okay, I'm on my way. I've got Seb Flude with me. He's hurt so get an ambulance there too. And any back-up you've got."

Now I could see panic in his face too. I could also feel blood on my cheek. I put up my hand and felt hair matted with dried blood but there was some fresh as well. "Yes," Ross said. "Hang on, though, Seb. Not long and there'll be an ambulance at your house." I saw a red traffic light, though we didn't stop at it, rain on the windscreen, and streetlights flashing past. I felt sick and detached. Then I guess that I lost consciousness, more or less. I certainly didn't remember the rest of the journey. At one stage, I felt a hand on my shoulder, though. "Wait here," a voice said. "Okay?"

"Yes," I mumbled. "Wait here." My eyes opened and there, in front of me, was my lime tree. Ross was creeping up our drive. I could hear nothing. The rain had stopped. My head was clear. I waited for a couple of minutes after Ross had disappeared from view, then scrambled painfully across the driver's seat and out into the quiet night. I would have loved to have lingered in the street, savouring the comforting familiarity of it all, but the drive and house beckoned. I wanted to go in but I was scared to do so. I had to force my legs to carry me up the drive.

The front door was slightly ajar. I peered round the gap but could see nothing. I couldn't hear anything either. I pushed open the door. No creaks and groans for atmosphere, I'm afraid. Just silence. The hallway was lit dimly by the glow that emanated from the partly open kitchen door. I faltered on the doorstep, gulped and willed myself forward. It felt like taking the final step into a darkened lions' den. The carpet under my feet felt very soft after my weeks on bare floorboards. It also deadened the noise of my movements. I derived reassurance from my noiselessness, I guess because I felt like a trespasser in my own house. On my left the cloakroom seemed deserted and on the right the studio door, unusually, was open. There didn't seem to be anyone inside, though. I inched my way down the hall, past the stairs. No light filtered down from the bedrooms so I carried on creeping towards the kitchen light.

To my right was the short corridor leading to the lounge. Right in front of me was the kitchen. I held my breath and gently pushed open the door. My eyes closed involuntarily. When they blinked open again I saw that the kitchen too was empty. I shook my head, exhaled and went back out into the hall. I stood there, inert, staring at the lounge door. Like the other, it was ajar. Ross must have taken a similar route through the house, opening doors and peering into each room in turn. A dim light only issued from the crack. Obviously the main lights were off but the pair of wall-lamps had been left on. Well, I thought to myself, it's either here or upstairs. Just walk in and find out. Get it over with. But it wasn't that easy. I just couldn't bring myself to walk four paces forward, push open a door and look inside a room. What was wrong with me? It was even my own lounge.

Suddenly the door opened and I nearly leapt out of my skin. It was Ross. For an instant, he wavered as well. Then he walked to me, put both his hands on my shoulders and forcibly turned me round. "No, Seb," he said, marching me back down the hallway with one of his arms round my shoulders. "Don't go in there."

"No!" I stopped walking and shouted, "I must!" I twisted out of his grasp and ran back down the corridor towards the lounge.

I stopped in the doorway, not daring to encroach on the room. It looked awful. Furniture scattered everywhere. The glass in the patio doors was smashed. They'd come in unnoticed from the wood at the back. There was a man I didn't recognize, presumably Mike the policeman, sprawled amongst the broken glass by the patio door. Mum was lying at one end of the room. I could only see her legs poking out from behind a chair. Dad was some distance away in the middle of the lounge, one arm entangled with the legs of an overturned chair. They weren't even lying together.

I doubt if I even jumped when Ross took me from behind and turned me around. I looked at him and cried, "They're not even together."

"No," he said, clearly lost for words.

"Put them together, Ross."

"No, Seb. I can't move them," he replied softly. "Come on, your ambulance will be waiting."

The last thing I saw as he led me away again was a slogan daubed in red on the back wall, "Grass screws you up."

Chapter 16

*It is neither fair nor reasonable to expect sadness
to confine itself to its causes. Like a river in flood,
when it subsides and the drowned bodies of
animals have been deposited in the treetops, there
is another kind of damage that must be considered;
the kind of damage that takes place beyond the torrent.*

You don't expect me to tell you how I felt at that
time, do you? Yes, of course you do. And Miss
Greene's encouraging me to bare my all as well.
The therapy of writing all this down requires it.
Well, here we go. I felt depressed, exhausted,
lonely, insecure, impoverished, confused, guilty,
bruised and broken. Towards other people I felt
little but hate and distrust. Most of the items on

my list are probably self-explanatory but perhaps a few need some expansion.

Guilt. I felt guilty because they got Mum and Dad, and not me. Why? Why didn't they come for me? After all, I was the major threat to Woodward. I tortured myself with the thought that his wrath would never have turned on Mum and Dad if I hadn't been rescued. I came to believe that their deaths were my fault. Why wasn't I killed? I did find an answer to this question eventually. All will be revealed. Well, this is the last chapter.

Distrust. I'd learned not to trust anyone. Certainly not girls bearing warm bras, policemen with routines, pleasant kidnappers, doctors, no one. Loneliness. No parents and no Lisa. No trust in humans, and not much hope. That's *real* poverty. At some point, someone (without a degree in diplomacy) told me that I'd inherited a fortune, but I regarded myself as impoverished. And hate. I hated the killers, Woodward, the rock music business, the drugs scene, scrap metal dealers, plastic cutlery, sinks, trees, everything and everyone. Girls meant nothing to me – abnormal response. Friends meant nothing to me – abnormal response. I didn't have much of a will to live, I guess. I didn't enjoy company, food, sleep – all abnormal responses.

That's how I came to enter Miss Greene's "school". To be weaned off drugs. To learn to live. To regain trust in human kind. And to dare to love again. They got me off drugs fairly quickly (and painfully) but learning to live, love and trust again took much longer. This act of writing down my story is part of the cure. It's supposed to clear out my system – like a good dose of diarrhoea – to rid myself of the last vestiges of abnormality. That's what Miss Greene said. She's no ordinary tutor, but you've probably guessed that already. She's a tutor-cum-psychiatrist, and her school is half full of headcases and half victims of crime (abused sons and daughters, rape victims, drugs addicts and the odd kidnap victim). Classes are half-lessons, half-therapy.

Did – does – this special school help me? Yes, but it took time. At the end of the kidnap I felt as if I'd had every layer of skin peeled off. I was raw. No matter how and where I was handled, it hurt. So at first the school didn't appear to be helping at all. The agony of losing my addiction only added to my soreness. But eventually even I noticed an improvement. For instance, despite the torture she put me through, I began to like Miss Greene. I still do. Even though she made me write all this, made me peel all my skin off once more. I'm raw again, but Miss Greene says, "Sometimes you have to open up a wound again to make it heal properly." I'm not sure that I feel fully healed, but she never promised me instant results or even a total recovery. And, of course, I haven't finished the story yet. I'd better tie up the loose ends right now.

They caught my doctor fairly quickly. They made me use my artistic skills to sketch him and then kept giving me doctors' photographs to look at – as and when my health let me. I looked at so many male doctors that they all seemed to merge into one. "No," I'd say. "He's like the last one. I said the nose was larger." Actually, though, I found that my mind could not be precise about his features. My memory seemed confused. "His eyebrows were darker and thicker, or perhaps less thick. I'm not sure." But when his photo really arrived, I knew. No hesitation at all. "That's him, Ross."

"Sure?"

"Sure. Bet he's got a Volvo."

Ross grinned. "You were right. He has. He's got a practice in Rotherham. Well, he has today. But he won't have tomorrow." He slapped me on the back, but gently, in deference to my health. "He didn't make a run for it – didn't think you'd be in a fit state to identify him. I'm glad he's a presumptuous bastard. Makes him easier to catch and a pleasure to prosecute."

It took a little longer to get Frank. If my faculties had been fully intact at the end of the kidnap, I might have aided his capture by deducing his real name. But they weren't, so I didn't. Anyway, the following episode was very important to me. It marked a distinct acceleration in the restoration of my faith in human kind.

First Miss Greene came in. "Seb," she said. "There's a couple of visitors for you. Sergeant Taylor and a colleague. You don't have to see them, if you don't want to."

"Oh? What's the problem with seeing Ross? He's been often enough."

"It's not so much Sergeant Taylor. It's what he wants to talk about. I've not allowed him to raise some topics till now. But I think you can cope now. It'll be good news and bad. It'll stir it all up again but . . . Well, what do you think?"

I shrugged. "If you think so."

"I'll send them in, then. Okay?"

He came in, sat on the bed and took a long look at me. "You're looking a bit better," he said.

"Thanks. But it's like saying, 'You've grown' to a child. Looking better's inevitable because I couldn't get any worse."

"True. Anyway, this is WPC Derbyshire. Emma." She smiled as she asked if she could sit on the spare chair. I nodded. "It's been a while," Ross said, clearly reluctant to get down to business. He glanced around the room, his eyes alighting on my guitar. "Still play it?" he asked, pointing at the guitar.

"Yes. Ever since your forensic chappies returned it. Sometimes it soothes, sometimes it makes me angry, but I enjoy it – and either way Miss Greene thinks it's useful therapy." Then I added, "It's my only relic of the kidnap, you know. Well, the only material one. I guess I could use any of Dad's guitars now. There's plenty of them, all better than that one. But somehow I think I'll stick with it. It's special to me, you see."

"I can understand that. But I have relics of the kidnap to worry about, as well. Arrests, for example."

"Oh? You mean Frank, or Woodward?"

"Both."

"But you know all about Woodward. Have you got him yet?"

"Prising people out of Brazil is not easy, Seb. He enjoys the benefits of Brazilian law, and the protection of some powerful traffickers."

"I suppose so."

"We will get him, though. But we're not talking weeks, Seb. We may not even be talking months. But, with a bit of international cooperation, we'll get him back."

"Do you think he's still in the drugs business? We did stop that, didn't we?"

Ross nodded. "We plugged one hole. The police alone can't solve the problem, though. We can keep a lid on some of it. That's all."

"What about the crack factory? Found it yet?"

"No. But it doesn't matter." Seeing the surprise in my face, he explained himself. "We've had a long look at all Woodward's premises, even ones distantly owned by his company, but couldn't locate it. It's out of commission, though, wherever it is. You see, they're cautious operators in this business. They'll assume that we did find it, that we're staking it out. They'll never return to it now. Anyway," he said, trying to buck up the conversation, "we're getting ahead of ourselves. I want Emma to have a chat with you. She conducted the interview with Lisa Woodward – remember – straight after you were kidnapped."

"Oh. You're the one," I said to the policewoman, "who thought she didn't lead me into a trap on purpose."

"What can I say, Seb? She was . . . nonplussed by it all. She was either a faithful girlfriend, or the world's worst bitch – and best actress."

"So why didn't she call the police? Shop her dad?"

"Did she have a reason to suspect him then?" Emma asked, leaping to Lisa's defence.

"I don't know. Maybe not at that time. But she did later. She must have known after she came to the hut."

Ross interrupted, saying, "Let's take this a step at a time, Seb. Stick with the time of the kidnap first."

I shrugged. "Okay. But in that case, we've already missed a step."

"How do you mean?" asked Ross.

"My minders were nobbled just before I was kidnapped."

"Yes. But we didn't learn anything from that. It was just a young lad. Succumbed to the offer of big money to steal a car and ram a blue Peugeot that was following your bus. He didn't know what he was getting into. What did you say Sh— Frank called such people? Secondary victims?"

"I see. So what's the next step?"

It was Ross that answered. "Lisa came to see your mum and dad."

"When?"

"A few days after. Before the excursion with her dog. I was with them, as protection, when she arrived. Just as well really. I had to make sure they didn't say too much. No drugs, no punishment angle. They didn't let on that it was anything more than blackmail. Besides, Lisa was assuming it was blackmail. She pleaded with them to pay a ransom to get you back." He paused, then added, "I agree with Emma. It was a convincing performance."

I really wanted to accept what they were trying to tell me about Lisa, but I was scared to do so. I didn't want to be disappointed later. She's a mystery to me, not yet confined to history. I opted for safer, less probing questions. "Why," I asked

Ross, "couldn't you tell her the truth? You must have known what was going on."

"The dealers wanted horror stories about punishment to get circulated. If someone messes around, they're going to lose an arm or a leg – or a relative – at the minimum. Not the sort of message we want to encourage. Such stories percolate enough without us confirming it to all and sundry."

"So Lisa didn't know about the drugs angle."

"No. Perhaps . . . Emma, would you take it from here?"

"She didn't know what her dad was into – neither did we – and she had no reason to link him to you. He'd never objected to her going out with you and in fact she thought he approved. There was nothing suspicious about that at the time but perhaps we know why now. A link to the Fludes proved very convenient. There was the argument on the night of the kidnap but show me a teenager who hasn't argued with parents about the time to be home. Not much significance there either."

"You seem very keen to protect her."

Emma smiled. "I wouldn't call it protection. We're keen to get to the truth, that's all. Anyway," she continued, "a few days later, she stopped going to school. She was signed off by her doctor."

"It wasn't my 'doctor', was it?"

"No." Emma smiled. "All above-board. A stress-related illness, he said. Shortly after, he gave his blessing to Woodward's plan to pack her off to relatives in the States, in the middle of nowhere. Peace and quiet was just what the doctor ordered. Better than a course of Valium."

I began to see a chink of light. "When was this?"

Emma shrugged. "Will a date mean anything to you? It was three weeks into your kidnap."

"I see."

"What are you thinking, Seb?" Ross asked.

"I wondered if it corresponded with her visit to the hut."

"So do we."

I couldn't help but speculate. "She found me, so her dad bundled her off before she could do him any damage. Do you think it's possible?"

Ross didn't answer straight away. Instead, he said, "There's more yet. Emma?"

Emma took a cassette tape out of her pocket. "We'd like you to listen to this. Can I put it in your cassette-player?" I nodded. I didn't dare ask what it was all about. I was too full of trepidation and a degree of hope that I thought was beyond me.

As Emma sorted out the tape, Ross continued, "If she was deliberately and quickly whisked out of the country after hearing you at the breaker's yard, she may not have had the opportunity to contact us about you. A very effective gag, I'd say. Anyway . . . Ready, Emma? Okay. Listen to this, Seb. It's not great quality so listen hard."

196

There were a few clicks, then a voice. I froze. It was eerie – and just a touch distressing. I hadn't heard his voice for so long. I didn't think I'd ever hear it again. I couldn't bear the thought of listening to an Afterglow album. But here he was, caught on tape.

"Hello. Sheffield 669252."

"Is that Pete Flude?"

My spine tingled. My head dropped. It had the advantage of hiding my face.

"Yes. Who's this?"

"I can't speak for long. It's about Seb. He's in Worksop. A scrap yard off Park Road."

"What?"

"I can't . . . Did you get what I said?"

"Yes. Worksop."

"I'm not . . ."

"Hello? Hello?"

There was a long pause, then another click. Emma turned off the cassette.

What was it that caused my floods of tears? Dad's voice? The tension or the relief? Or was it the sound of Lisa's voice? A new-found belief in her innocence? The proof that she had saved me? Whatever it was, I cried and cried and couldn't stop. A kind of delirium, I guess. Ross and Emma had to call Miss Greene to sort me out. She stayed with me for the rest of the interview.

"We wanted you to hear it some time ago, but . . .

it was thought wise not to," Ross said. Miss Greene smiled as if her ban on the tape had been vindicated.

"Why did you want me to hear it?"

"We have to have your identification of the voice. Not prejudiced by hearing any guesses we may have made. Guess is all we can do."

"Well, you guessed right. It's Lisa."

"Beyond all reasonable doubt?" Seeing me frown, Ross smiled. "I have to ask. It wasn't a good line. Probably an international call."

"It *was* Lisa. You think she evaded her minders for a minute. Enough to make the call."

"That's right. We also thought you might welcome hearing who gave us the tip-off. Thought it might help you clarify things."

"You . . . er . . . You thought right." I took a deep breath, sighed and then sobbed again. I didn't really mind disgracing myself in front of an audience. Miss Greene's therapy had dispelled any associated shame. At times during my cure I was intensely emotional. I would burst into tears listening to a sad song, listening to a really good song, or watching a silly sentimental programme on the box. When I wasn't being emotional, I was hard, mean and moody. I snapped at everyone or said nothing at all. But after the tape . . . My attitude improved. She hadn't betrayed me after all! Her dad had not forced her into an unwanted relationship with me. She'd given the police the lead they needed to rescue me! She wasn't part of Woodward Drugs Company.

"You think she made the call from the States?" I asked.

"Presumably. The delays between exchanges are right for it."

"And now she's in Brazil with her parents?"

"Yes."

"Surely they're keeping her against her will. Can't you get her out?"

Ross shrugged. "No promises. But we'll try. We'll have to get a message to her. If she can get to the British Embassy, we can take it from there. Otherwise . . . it's a problem. As I said, Seb, no promises."

I nodded. "I know you'll do your best." I paused before asking another question, because I still didn't understand it all. "Why did she go to the hut? Something must have made her suspicious."

"Now that we don't know. But perhaps your Frank can help us."

"Frank?"

"Take a look at this photo," said Ross, handing it to me. "Can you tell me who it is?"

Did I recognize the impish face? I'd never forget it. I nodded to Ross and handed it back. I didn't want to look at him more than I had to. "Yes, it's him."

"The man you knew as Frank?"

"How did you get him?"

"We haven't. He's gone to ground. But we know who he is now. Your doctor was very anxious to cooperate," Ross said. "Given the charges against him, I'm not surprised. He knows that judges bear cooperation in mind when sentencing."

"So you're going to track Frank down?"

"We're going to try. His name, by the way," he said, tapping the photograph, "is Shankly. Paul Shankly."

I hesitated, then murmured, "Yes. Of course." I was talking to myself, but I said it aloud.

"What?"

"'Frankly, Mr Shankly'. He knew the song. He quoted from it. He named himself 'Frank' after it."

"I'll take your word for it," Ross said, clearly a little lost. "Anyway, he caught Lisa at the scrap yard, no doubt. Perhaps he found out why she went there. We only have to find *him*."

"Another question."

"Yes?"

"Woodward had made a run for it before your man got to him that night. Right?" Ross nodded. "Why?" I asked. "How did he know you were on to him?"

"I can only guess. I think his American friends phoned, telling him they'd discovered Lisa making her call. He must have assumed that she'd blown it sky high by giving her name – or his. I don't know, but he certainly packed his bags pretty quickly. Though he would have had contingency plans already in place, no doubt. As soon as you rumbled him, he'd have been figuring out an escape route – just in case."

I shuddered as I continued the logic. "Is that why he didn't kill me? Because he thought that Lisa had spilled the beans anyway? So my knowledge wasn't the big threat any more?"

"It fits, doesn't it?" Ross glanced at Miss Greene, as if to ask for permission before he continued. "He receives the information in that phone call, knows that your parents would be left at the house with less than full protection, and . . . takes advantage of it. If he'd thought you were the only one that knew the truth about him, he'd have sent the hitmen to the hut, not to your house."

Miss Greene was smiling sympathetically at me. She knew the guilt-ridden agonies that I'd gone through. "Woodward made the decision to switch the punishment to your mum and dad – on the basis of the phone call from the States," she said firmly. "It wasn't your fault, or anything you did. And it wasn't because you were rescued. He exploited the circumstances of your rescue, that's all. Okay? It was Woodward."

"Yes," I said. "I understand."

I guess that, on balance, I felt happy that day. Happy to shed some guilt. Very happy to learn of

Lisa. In fact, delighted to learn of Lisa. It renewed hope and the will to live. I could look back with less hate and anger. I didn't derive much pleasure from hearing that the net was closing around Frank. I had no thirst for revenge. Besides, Frank seemed to me to be the best of a bad bunch. I doubt if he signed death warrants or made decisions about the treatment of the sons of rock stars. There was a negative aspect to the day. The conversation made me concerned about Lisa. Worried about how she was being treated. Yet I could do little but keep my fingers crossed for her.

Five months on. In comes Ross yet again. More news of Frank. (To me he was still Frank. I couldn't get used to calling him Paul Shankly.) "Well," Ross began, "he's behind bars, as they say."

"Oh?" I still couldn't show much enthusiasm, but I was curious. "Where was he? Some remote Scottish island?"

"No. A stranger stands out too much in small communities. It's far easier to become invisible in London. But we got him in Manchester. He made the mistake of turning up at a hospital where his mother is ill."

"Has he told you anything interesting?"

"He claims that he was going to refuse to carry on holding or doping you into oblivion. Do you have any comment on that? Anything that would back up his story?"

I sighed. "I don't know, Ross. It was a long time ago, and recognizing reality was not my strong point. I had several conversations with Lisa when, in fact, she was in the States. I do remember that he was concerned about me, though. He seemed genuine. He stopped me really hurting myself. The old head banging, if you recall. And . . . er . . . yes, he did walk out at the end. He said something like, 'If Woodward wants to complete this job, he can do it himself.' He left, he said, to make a report."

"Okay. That figures," Ross replied. "You see, Shankly maintains that he went to see Woodward but found the whole place in turmoil. Woodward in a right old temper, moving out and issuing contracts left, right and centre. Shankly confirms that Woodward had got word from the States about Lisa's phone call, but he also says that he persuaded Woodward not to harm you further. He says he pointed out the futility of further action against you."

"You mean, he convinced Woodward that Lisa would have told all in her phone call?"

"That's what he says. He's trying to play your guardian angel."

Conspiracies by both Lisa and Frank had kept me alive! How many more baddies were going to turn into goodies? "Why did he do it?" I asked.

"Take your side? When I asked him, all he said was, 'Seb Flude was just a kid'."

"Meaning?"

"Meaning he was too scared to be responsible for a teenager's fate. Or maybe he had enough scruples to believe that it was wrong to involve you in their very adult business. Or maybe he's dreamed up the whole episode – he's had plenty of time to think – knowing it'll go down well with a jury."

"Mm. But it all rings true, doesn't it?"

Ross nodded. "He also protested about Lisa's treatment – or so he says." Then he added, "I believe him, actually, because he seems to have a soft spot for her."

"You don't mean they had some sort of relationship?"

"No. He speaks fondly of her, that's all. As if he admired her, and what she did. Kindred spirits, you see, both turning against Woodward."

"Did he know why Lisa went to the hut?"

"No. Or he's not letting on."

"Pity." I sighed. "Any news of her, Ross?"

"Sorry, Seb."

I hope that you're not holding your breath, waiting for Lisa's reappearance in this story, expecting her to fling open the door at any moment, dash across the room, and engage me madly and passionately on the bed. Happy endings aren't my strong point.

There was news of her eventually, though. Not great news, but not bad. Just news. But before I give it to you, you're going to have to cast your mind back. Remember that the police in the States had a mole in the American end of the drugs racket? Well, they did. And this chap, bless him, had been working at getting close to the Woodwards so as to get the message about the British Embassy through to Lisa. "It's tricky," Ross explained, "without blowing his cover."

"Okay, he's a saint. Just tell me the news, Ross," I replied.

"He doesn't mind being a saint, but he doesn't want to become a martyr. Don't forget that if he opens up with Lisa, he reveals his true motives and jeopardizes the whole operation. In effect, he has to trust her with his life. That," said Ross, "is asking a lot."

"Come on, Ross. I can tell he's already done it. Stop the big build-up and give me the story."

"I see that your powers of perception have returned. All right," he conceded. "But don't raise your hopes too much. I haven't got a lot."

"Anything."

"Our man got a quiet word with her. Which means that he does trust her. Because she doesn't fit, because she's not free. Anyway, he found out why she first suspected . . ."

"Ross," I interrupted. "Let's take this a step at a

time. The important things first. Just tell me, is she okay? You know, safe."

Ross smiled. "I'm sorry. It's my tidy mind trying to complete the picture. She's fine. Not happy, of course, but she was pleased to hear that you're back in the land of the living. She seemed healthy, not maltreated. She has tutors at the house. They're minders really. She's watched quite closely. But at least she's now aware of how to escape. It won't be easy for her, and it's not.free from risk if she tries it."

Which is the better life? Safe and unhappy, or a dangerous dash to freedom? No doubt Lisa will decide. I have no right, and no means, to influence her.

"Is that all? Just police business left?"

"No." He removed a piece of paper from his pocket. "There's this. She scribbled a note to you. This is a copy. I have to have the original for files." He handed it over. My hand shook as I took it from him.

Seb, I am very sorry. Your poor parents. I'm relieved that you're well, though. After the police spoke to me about your kidnap, I went to see your mum and dad. They were lovely to me, Seb. I can't tell you how privileged and proud you should feel about them. They were really proud of you too. Your mum said, "He can always raise a smile, our Seb. And that helps him cope. I think he'll see this through." I can't think of them without crying.

I tried to be loyal to my dad, Seb, just like you. He was a good dad to me. I didn't want to believe that he might have bad points. But you were right. Fathers have good points and bad. Mine's no different. It came as a real shock when I overheard him say to Mr Shankly, "I don't think our business at Worksop can be terminated for the moment. Flude is hardly sweating yet." It took a while to sink in. I knew Paul Shankly had always fancied me, by the way he used to look at me, so I chatted him up to try and get information from him. No joy, so I went to the only place I knew in Worksop – Dad's breaker's yard. You know the rest, I think.

No time to write any more. I wish I could see you. Then I could explain it all properly. And I'd say sorry again and again. You may not want to see a Woodward ever again, but I like to think you'd give me a chance. I don't know if I'll be able to get away, but I'll try. I promise. Till then, keep well. Love, Lisa.

I put the letter on the bed and breathed deeply. It's difficult to describe what I felt about the note. How would the Second Coming feel to a Christian?

"Well?" Ross reminded me that he was still in

the room. "You want me to leave you to it?"

"That's probably best. But," I added before he left, "how do I get a reply to her?"

"You don't. Our man got away with it this time. Mission accomplished. It's up to her now. He's not going to risk it again."

"Okay. I see the point. He's forever in my good books anyway. I hope he gets a fat bonus for this," I said, indicating Lisa's note. "He can use me as a reference any time."

Things have looked up for me since the letter. Lisa hasn't returned yet but I wake each morning thinking, "Well, it probably won't be today either, but there again . . ." In writing this novel, I've stirred up those old feelings of hate and grief but learned to ease the pain as I always used to do – with a bit of humour. The art of smiling and joking have come back to me (hopefully you've noticed it in the story), even if it is used as a device to protect me from unwanted emotions.

So what's changed in the world since the kidnap? Throughout the writing of this novel, Miss Greene's been trying to get me to take an interest in the world outside my own. Perhaps it was more therapy than a literary device, but now I'm hooked on it anyway. If Lisa does return, I won't be meeting her outside Virgin Records in High Street. I'm told that the shop isn't there any more. Pity. The

Smiths, Dad's tip for the top, have split up. Though in the spirit of change, he'd have probably approved of the break-up. Compact discs have almost taken over from vinyl, it seems. You can even buy the best of Afterglow on CD now, tastefully called "Pete Flude's Afterglow". I told you – you really need a sense of humour in this world. What else might I mention? Oh, yes. You do read reports of crack in the country but there was a lull for a time. Even now, it's only a trickle compared to the problem in the USA. The floodgates are still closed, it seems. Ross tells me that crack accounts for less than one per cent of all drug seizures. And they're not huge amounts either. Perhaps there's a little something for the Fludes to be proud of.

So that's it. The end of my story. So much for the past. What about my future? Miss Greene has, with much glee and flourish, just announced that this novel has earned me remission. Soon I'll be able to become part of the big outside world whose events I've been reporting as if they were totally isolated from me. But what will I do in it? I can definitely say that I won't become a novelist. I only had one story that I wanted to tell, and that's over. Despite my attempted rebellion against parental precedent, I've found that my first love is for music. During my trials and tribulations, music sustained me. Propped by the side of my desk where I'm scribbling this conclusion is my guitar.

Perhaps if I put in a bit more effort and practice
. . . I might even try again to write my own songs.
It could be that they'll sustain me in the future, I
don't know. We'll see. But if I'm going to have a
shot at it, I suppose that I'd better start right here.
Try this for size.

When the war was over
There was not one hero
Only villains and a dreadful emptiness
So he filled his time recounting all his losses
On plain white leaves, no more than dead trees.

He'd no sense of revenge
There's no sense in revenge
He filled his scrapbook with the scraps of his life
It somehow revived those loved and taken by knife
It eased the pain, he could smile again.

Much reason for sorrow
But maybe tomorrow
She'll return and see him again.
He shouted aloud his defiance at life
It seemed to revive those loved and taken by knife.

That's your lot. It's a wrap.
Good day, sports.

Look out for other exciting titles from
Malcolm Rose – the master of suspense . . .

The Highest Form of Killing
All is quiet at Crookland Bay – site of a top secret MoD research station – then the accidents start to happen . . .

Son of Pete Flude
Seb is the son of Pete Flude – international rockstar and sex symbol. It sounds like an easy ride . . . but is it?

P●INT CRiME

The Smoking Gun
When David Rabin is found dead, his sister is determined to find the murderer. But what is the "smoking gun" – the lethal poison which killed him?

Concrete Evidence
When the Keatings make the macabre discovery of their mother's body, they vow to find her killer and avenge her murder . . .

adlib...

The Obtuse Experiment
What happens when the holiday of alifetime turns into a nightmare you can't escape?

THE UNDERWORLD TRILOGY
Peter Beere

When life became impossible for the homeless of London many left the streets to live beneath the earth. They made their homes in the corridors and caves of the Underground. They gave their home a name. They called it UNDERWORLD.

UNDERWORLD
It was hard for Sarah to remember how long she'd been down there, but it sometimes seemed like forever. It was hard to remember a life on the outside. It was hard to remember the real world. Now it seemed that there was nothing but creeping on through the darkness, there was nothing but whispering and secrecy.

And in the darkness lay a man who was waiting to kill her . . .

UNDERWORLD II
"Tracey," she called quietly. No one answered. There was only the dark threatening void which forms Underworld. It's a place people can get lost in, people can disappear in. It's not a place for young girls whose big sisters have deserted them. Mandy didn't know what to do. She didn't know what had swept her sister and her friends from Underworld. All she knew was that Tracey had gone off and left her on her own.

UNDERWORLD III
Whose idea was it? Emma didn't know and now it didn't matter anyway. It was probably Adam who had said, "Let's go down and look round the Underground." It was something to tell their friends about, something new to try. To boast that they had been inside the secret Underworld, a place no one talked about, but everyone knew was there.

It had all seemed like a great adventure, until they found the gun . . .

Also by Peter Beere

CROSSFIRE
When Maggie runs away from Ireland, she finds herself roaming the streets of London destitute and alone. But Maggie has more to fear then the life of a runaway. Her step-father is an important member of the IRA – and if he doesn't find her before his enemies do, Maggie might just find herself caught up in the crossfire . . .

Point

Pointing the way forward

More compelling reading from top authors.

The Highest Form of Killing
Malcolm Rose
Death is in the very air . . .

Seventeenth Summer
K.M. Peyton
*Patrick Pennington – mean, moody and out
of control . . .*

Secret Lives
William Taylor
*Two people drawn together by their mysterious
pasts . . .*

Flight 116 is Down
Caroline B. Cooney
Countdown to disaster . . .

Forbidden
Caroline B. Cooney
Theirs was a love that could never be . . .

Hostilities
Caroline Macdonald
*In which the everyday throws shadows of another,
more mysterious world . . .*

Encounter worlds where men and women make hazardous voyages through space; where time travel is a reality and the fifth dimension a possibility; where the ultimate horror has already happened and mankind breaks through the barrier of technology . . .

The Obernewtyn Chronicles:
Book 1: Obernewtyn
Book 2: The Farseekers
Isobelle Carmody

A new breed of humans are born into a hostile world struggling back from the brink of apocalypse . . .

Random Factor
Jessica Palmer

Battle rages in space. War has been erased from earth and is now controlled by an all-powerful computer – until a random factor enters the system . . .

First Contact
Nigel Robinson

In 1992 mankind launched the search for extra-terrestial intelligence. Two hundred years later, someone responded . . .

Virus
Molly Brown

A mysterious virus is attacking the staff of an engineering plant . . . Who, or *what* is responsible?

Look out for:

Strange Orbit
Margaret Simpson

Scatterlings
Isobelle Carmody

Body Snatchers
Stan Nicholls

Read Point SF and enter a new dimension . . .

Point Romance

If you like Point Horror, you'll love Point Romance!

Anyone can hear the language of love.

**Are you burning with passion, and aching with desire?
Then these are the books for you! Point Romance brings
you passion, romance, heartache . . . and *love*.**

Available now:

**First Comes Love:
To Have and to Hold
For Better, For Worse
In Sickness and in Health
Till Death Do Us Part**
Jennifer Baker

A Winter Love Story
Jane Claypool Miner

Two Weeks in Paradise
Denise Colby

**Saturday Night
Last Dance
New Year's Eve
Summer Nights**
Caroline B. Cooney

**Cradle Snatcher
Kiss Me, Stupid**
Alison Creaghan

Summer Dreams, Winter Love
Mary Francis Shura

The Last Great Summer
Carol Stanley

Lifeguards:
**Summer's Promise
Summer's End**
Todd Strasser

French Kiss
Robyn Turner

Look out for:

Crazy About You
Robyn Turner

Spotlight on Love
Denise Colby

***Last Summer, First Love:*
A Time to Love
Goodbye to Love**
Jennifer Baker